Big Bucks . . .

"I have a surprise for Steven and the girls," Aunt Helen announced. "I wanted to do something nice for the three of you. I didn't know what sort of gift you would like so I did this instead." She took three envelopes out of her pocketbook and handed them to Steven, Jessica, and Elizabeth. "Go ahead, open them," she said.

Elizabeth broke the seal on her envelope and peered inside. She couldn't believe what she saw! The envelope was stuffed full of money!

"Wow!" Jessica cried. She took the money out and counted it. "It's a hundred dollars!"

Bantam Skylark Books in the SWEET VALLEY TWINS AND FRIENDS series
Ask your bookseller for the books you have missed

SWEET VALLEY TWINS
AND FRIENDS

The Wakefields Strike It Rich

Written by
Jamie Suzanne

Created by
FRANCINE PASCAL

A BANTAM SKYLARK BOOK
NEW YORK · TORONTO · LONDON · SYDNEY · AUCKLAND

RL 4, 008–012

THE WAKEFIELDS STRIKE IT RICH
A Bantam Skylark Book / February 1992

*Sweet Valley High® and Sweet Valley Twins and Friends are
trademarks of Francine Pascal*

Conceived by Francine Pascal

*Produced by Daniel Weiss Associates, Inc.
33 West 17th Street
New York, NY 10011*

Cover art by James Mathewuse

ISBN 0-553-15950-X

Published simultaneously in the United States and Canada

*Bantam Books are published by Bantam Books, a division of Bantam
Doubleday Dell Publishing Group, Inc. Its trademark, consisting of the
words "Bantam Books" and the portrayal of a rooster, is Registered in U.S.
Patent and Trademark Office and in other countries. Marca Registrada.
Bantam Books, 666 Fifth Avenue, New York, New York 10103.*

PRINTED IN THE UNITED STATES OF AMERICA

OPM   0 9 8 7 6 5 4 3 2 1

To Caitlin Walsh

One

◇

"Elizabeth, wait up!" Jessica Wakefield called to her twin sister from the front steps of Sweet Valley Middle School.

Elizabeth turned around.

"You're not crazy enough to be going home now, are you?" Jessica asked, catching up to her sister on the sidewalk.

"What are you talking about, Jess? Why wouldn't I go home?"

"Aunt Helen's coming tonight," Jessica reminded her sister.

"I know. I can't wait to see her," Elizabeth replied.

"Neither can I, but you know what always happens before anyone comes to visit. Mom and Dad make us *clean*."

"But we just cleaned the *whole* house this

weekend." As punishment for the party they had thrown while their parents were in Mexico, Jessica, Elizabeth, and their fourteen-year-old brother, Steven, had to clean up the house for their great-aunt's visit.

"Trust me, they'll think of something. We'll have to polish the silver or wax the floors. There's no way I'm going home before Aunt Helen gets there."

"So what are you going to do?" Elizabeth asked.

"A bunch of us are going to Casey's," Jessica said. "Do you want to come?"

Elizabeth smiled. "You only want me to go so you won't get into trouble."

"No, that's not it," Jessica said, even though her sister was right. If neither one of them showed up until dinner, then Jessica figured she'd only get in half as much trouble. "I just think it would be fun to hang out at Casey's. A lot more fun than what Mom's probably got in store for us."

"You have a point," Elizabeth said. "OK, I'll go."

"Great!" Jessica said. "I'm supposed to meet everyone out here on the front steps."

"I can't believe *you're* here before everyone else," Elizabeth commented. "Usually you're the last one to get anywhere!"

Jessica smiled. Elizabeth was right—Jessica

did have a habit of being late. But it wasn't her fault. She had been born four minutes after Elizabeth, and she had been showing up later than her sister ever since.

That wasn't the only difference between them, either. Jessica liked to do things on the spur of the moment, while Elizabeth planned things in advance. Jessica belonged to the Unicorns, a group of the prettiest and most popular girls at Sweet Valley Middle School. She was also a member of the Boosters, the middle school's cheering squad. Jessica's main interests were clothes and boys.

Elizabeth was only interested in one boy— Todd Wilkins, whom she had been going out with for a few months. She spent a lot of her time working on the *Sweet Valley Sixers*, the sixth-grade newspaper, or hanging out with Amy Sutton, her closest friend after Jessica.

Despite all their differences, however, Elizabeth and Jessica were best friends, and they shared everything—from thoughts to clothes to their identical long blond hair and blue-green eyes.

"*Here* you are," Lila Fowler said, walking out of the school. Mary Wallace, Janet Howell, Mandy Miller, and Brooke Dennis were following her.

"Where did you think I'd be?" Jessica said.

"We said we'd meet at my locker," Lila said.

"No, we didn't," Jessica insisted. "We said we'd meet out here."

"No, that was the original plan, but then we—"

"Oh, who cares," Janet Howell interrupted. "We're all here, right?"

Jessica sighed. "Right!" Even though Lila was her best friend after Elizabeth, they argued all the time. "What are we waiting for?"

As the girls went on their way, Elizabeth tapped Jessica on the shoulder and whispered in her ear. "I hope Steven is having fun polishing the silver!"

"Uh-oh. It looks like Steven had the same idea," Elizabeth said when they walked into Casey's twenty minutes later. Steven was sitting at a large table with several friends, including Joe Howell, Janet's older brother.

"Well, at least all three of us are in this together," Jessica said. She looked over at Steven's table. "Who's that girl with the blond hair? I've never seen her before."

"Beats me." Elizabeth pulled out a chair and sat down.

"That's Jill somebody-or-other," Janet said.

Jessica craned her neck to get a better look at Jill. From what she could see, Steven was staring at Jill with an incredibly dumb look on his face.

Jessica sat down next to Elizabeth. "Steven looks like he has a *major* crush on that girl."

"He is kind of staring at her," Elizabeth said.

"He hasn't even noticed that we're here yet!" Jessica said. "This is great. We can spy on him and then make fun of him later."

"What are you guys talking about?" Lila asked, taking some menus from behind the napkin holder. She passed them around the table.

Jessica pointed to Steven.

"My brother Joe told me that he likes Jill, too," Janet said. "No offense, but I don't think Steven stands a chance with her, not with Joe around."

Jessica frowned. It was just like Janet to imply that her brother was better than theirs. "You might be surprised," she said. "I mean, Steven's had lots of girlfriends."

"Yeah, but she looks like she really likes Joe," Janet said. "I bet they'll be a couple soon."

Jessica looked thoughtful. "I don't know, Janet. Steven can be a real Romeo when he tries."

"OK, so there I was, trying to do this problem on the board, and I must have been up there for, like, five minutes. When I finally finished it, I turned around—and old Quigley was *asleep*!"

Everyone at the table burst out laughing.

"Joe, you crack me up," Jill Hale said.

"I can't believe that really happened," Larry Harris said.

"It's true. The whole class started to crack up, and Quigley jumped up and made some lame excuse about how he'd been up late the night before correcting our homework," Joe said.

"Yeah, right," Steven said. "He was probably watching professional wrestling on TV." He smiled at Jill, but she didn't laugh.

"Hey, did you see that new show, 'Staying Up With Bob'?" Joe asked.

"Yeah, I really like it," Jill replied.

"Me, too," Steven hurried to add. "My favorite part is when he goes around the audience and makes fun of people." He looked hopefully at Jill.

"Yeah, that's OK," Joe said. "But the best part is the stupid stunts."

Jill nodded. "Definitely."

"Hey, did you see the guy who dribbled a basketball with his chin?" Joe asked.

Jill laughed. "He looked like a complete idiot!"

Steven sat back in his chair. He *felt* like a complete idiot. He kept trying to impress Jill, or at least get into a conversation with her, but she was acting as if he were invisible.

It's all Joe's fault, Steven thought. When it came to girls, Steven felt that Joe took over every conversation. Girls always laughed at Joe's jokes, and it seemed that he could talk to them easily. Steven, meanwhile, always ended up feeling like a fool.

Steven thought that if he could spend some time alone with Jill, he could really get to know her, and she would see that he wasn't an idiot, after all. But that meant asking her for a date. Steven didn't know if he was up to that. If she turned him down, he'd be totally humiliated.

He looked at Jill, who was smiling at something Joe had just said.

I will ask her out! Steven thought. *I'll sweep her off her feet—Jill Hale won't know what hit her!*

"That was the best hot fudge sundae I ever had," Mary Wallace said as she dropped her spoon into the empty dish.

Brooke Dennis hit her playfully on the arm. "You always say that."

Jessica licked her spoon. "I think butterscotch is the best."

The waitress put their bill on the table, and Janet picked it up. "Since we all got sundaes, we all owe the same amount. The bill is fourteen dollars, so it's two dollars each."

"Plus we have to leave a couple of dollars for a tip," Lila reminded her. "Daddy says you should always leave twenty percent. But then again this isn't exactly the kind of restaurant we usually go to," she added.

Jessica turned to Elizabeth and rolled her eyes. Lila never missed a chance to remind everyone of how rich she was.

"OK, so we each owe about two fifty," Elizabeth said.

Each girl started to get her money out of her bag. Jessica reached into her jeans pocket. She pulled out two quarters. Then she opened her backpack and took out her wallet. "Oops," she muttered, looking inside.

"Oops what?" Elizabeth said.

"How much money do you have?" Jessica asked.

"I have just enough to cover me," Elizabeth said. "Why, don't you have any money?"

Jessica shook her head.

"Jessica, how could you order ice cream if you knew you couldn't pay for it?" Elizabeth asked.

"I thought I had two dollars in here," Jessica said. "I could have sworn I—" Jessica suddenly remembered where her two dollars had gone. She had spent them the day before on hair ribbons.

Lila counted up the money on the table. "We're two fifty short," she said.

Jessica put her fifty cents in the center of the table.

"Is that all you have?" Lila asked.

Jessica nodded. "Can you put in two dollars for me?"

"You mean, can you *borrow* it from me?"

Jessica didn't see why Lila had to make a big thing of it. It wasn't as if Lila couldn't spare a measly two dollars. "Or you could just buy my sundae this time," Jessica said.

"Jessica, money doesn't grow on trees, you know," Lila said with a frown. "I have an allowance, too."

"Yeah, and it's about five times bigger than mine," Jessica said.

"That's not the point." Lila opened her purse and took out two dollars. "I have to keep track of my money just like you do. I'll *lend* you the money, but I want you to pay me back as soon as you can. Promise?"

Jessica sighed. "I promise."

"You know, you should really learn how to manage your money," Lila said. "You're always running out of it."

"That's because I don't *have* any," Jessica complained.

"I'll bet that even if you did, you'd still be broke all the time," Lila said with a smirk.

"Well, if I did have money, I'd be a *lot* more generous to my friends," Jessica said angrily.

Lila pointed at the floor. "Oh, Jessica, there's

a penny. Maybe you should grab it before someone else does!" Then Janet, Mary, Brooke, and
Mandy all started laughing.

Jessica felt her face turn bright pink. She'd
had all the teasing she could take from Lila. Somehow she would show her!

Two

◇

Elizabeth ran into the living room and threw her arms around her great-aunt. "Aunt Helen! It's so great to see you!" Suddenly, she stepped back. "Oh, no—are you OK?"

Aunt Helen held up her right arm, which was covered in a white plaster cast. "You mean this silly thing?"

"What happened?" Elizabeth asked worriedly.

"Oh, it's nothing. I just had a little accident." Aunt Helen smiled. "You look wonderful. How long has it been since I last saw you? I think you must be at least a foot taller and—well, hello, Jessica!"

"Hi!" Jessica walked over and kissed Aunt Helen on the cheek. "Did you break your arm?"

"Sort of," Aunt Helen replied. "Don't worry, it doesn't hurt."

"Can we sign your cast?" Jessica asked eagerly.

"Sure, if you'd like to." Aunt Helen sat down on the couch and patted the cushions on either side of her. "While you do that, you can tell me everything you've been up to lately."

Jessica flopped down beside Aunt Helen. "Did I tell you that I met Coco? It was so exciting. She actually came to our house—can you believe it?"

"Not exactly," Aunt Helen replied, looking puzzled. "Who is Coco?"

Jessica giggled. "She's only the best singer in the world. And she also happens to be our friend Brooke Dennis's mom. You should see her videos. They're so cool."

Elizabeth smiled at the thought of her great-aunt watching music videos. Aunt Helen was sixty-four years old. She had plenty of energy, but she wasn't exactly up-to-date on things. She liked old movies and Frank Sinatra.

"Anyway, we went to one of her concerts," Jessica said.

"How exciting," Aunt Helen said. "Are you still working on the newspaper, Elizabeth?"

Elizabeth nodded. "I really like it."

"I can't wait until you grow up and become a famous writer," Aunt Helen said. "I'll be able to tell all my friends that I know a celebrity!" She winked at Jessica.

A few minutes later, the front door opened. Mr. and Mrs. Wakefield walked into the living room, with Steven right behind them. "Look who we found in the driveway," Mrs. Wakefield said.

Aunt Helen got up from the couch and held out her arms. "Let me look at this handsome young man!"

Steven blushed and kicked the carpet with his shoe. "Hi."

Aunt Helen went over to Steven and gave him a hug. "I can't believe how grown up all of you are!"

"Well, some of us are," Steven said, frowning at Jessica. She stuck her tongue out at him.

"Do we still have some time before dinner?" Aunt Helen asked. "I have a surprise for Steven and the girls."

"Certainly," Mr. Wakefield said. "We won't eat for another hour or so."

"Good. Now, I want you all to sit down," Aunt Helen instructed them. "You too, Ned and Alice. I'll be right back." She went into the den, which had been fixed up as a bedroom for her visit.

Aunt Helen came back in carrying a large pocketbook. She sat down, placing it on her lap. "I wanted to do something nice for the three of you. I was thinking of bringing you something, but I wasn't sure what you'd like. So I decided to do this instead." Aunt Helen took three envelopes out of her pocketbook and handed them to Steven, Jessica, and Elizabeth. "Go ahead, open them," she said.

Elizabeth broke the seal on her envelope and peered inside. She couldn't believe what she saw! The envelope was stuffed full of money!

"Wow!" Jessica cried. She took the money out and counted it. "It's a hundred dollars!"

"A hundred dollars?" Elizabeth murmured in disbelief.

"Hey, thanks, Aunt Helen," Steven said. He fanned the ten-dollar bills and waved them in the air. "This is going to come in *very* handy."

Aunt Helen smiled. "I thought it might."

"Helen, you didn't have to bring anything," Mrs. Wakefield said. "You know that."

"This is very generous of you," Mr. Wakefield added. He looked a bit shocked.

"Is there something special you had in mind for the kids?" Mrs. Wakefield asked.

Aunt Helen shook her head. "I want them to use the money however they want."

"Excellent!" Steven said.

"Thank you so much, Aunt Helen," Elizabeth said. "This really is a big surprise."

"You don't know how great this is," Jessica

said. "I mean, this is the best thing that's happened to me in a long time."

Aunt Helen laughed. "Better than meeting Coco?"

"Maybe you three should think about putting it in your savings accounts," Mrs. Wakefield said.

Jessica turned to Elizabeth and mouthed, "No way!"

"Yes, that sounds like a very good idea," Mr. Wakefield said. "You could put it toward your college education. If you deposit it in the bank now, it'll earn lots of interest by the time you need it for college."

"Dad, that's six years from now," Jessica complained. "Why would I want to do that?"

"Your father's right—you could decide to save this money," Aunt Helen said. "But I didn't give it to you so you could just put it in the bank. Spend it however you like. Of course, if you decide to save it, that's fine, too. But I want that decision to be completely up to you."

"I've been saving up for a camera lately," Elizabeth told her. "This will really help."

"Perfect!" Aunt Helen said. "What about you, Jessica? Did you have something special in mind?"

"I'm going to *spend* it!"

Aunt Helen laughed. "Good. And I hope you enjoy it."

"Thanks again, Aunt Helen," Elizabeth said. "This is really nice of you."

"Yeah, thanks," Steven added.

Jessica leaned over and kissed Aunt Helen on the cheek. "Thank you, thank you, thank you!" she cried.

"You know, if the three of you put your money together, you could—" Mr. Wakefield began.

"Dad!" Jessica and Steven yelled.

Mr. Wakefield grinned and held up his hands. "All right, I'll stop making suggestions. You three spend your money any way you want. Just don't spend it all in one day!"

"A hundred dollars? I don't think so," Steven replied.

"Even I couldn't do that," Jessica said.

"Want to bet?" Mrs. Wakefield said with a smile.

As soon as everybody finished eating dinner, Jessica ran upstairs to call Lila.

"Lila, you are *not* going to believe what happened," Jessica said when her friend picked up the phone.

"You found some more change on the way home?" Lila said.

"Ha ha," Jessica said. "You're not even close."

"OK, so what happened?" Lila asked.

"You know my great-aunt is visiting, right? We heard even before she got here that she had a big surprise for us," Jessica explained. "Then tonight she handed us a hundred dollars!" *Take that, Lila*, she was thinking.

"So you have to split it three ways, right?" Lila said.

"No way!" Jessica said. "She gave each of us a hundred. Can you believe it? I'm rich!"

"Not really," Lila said. "I mean, that's a lot of money, but it's not like you won the lottery or anything."

Jessica rolled her eyes. Lila was the only person she knew who wouldn't be impressed by a hundred dollars. To her, it was small change! "I think it's a lot of money," she told Lila. "Think of all the things I can buy now!"

"After you pay me back, that is," Lila said.

"Don't worry, you'll get your lousy two dollars," Jessica snapped. Lila really knew how to ruin the moment.

"It wasn't a lousy two dollars this afternoon," Lila said. "I mean, if I hadn't loaned you that money, you'd probably still be at Casey's, washing dishes to pay if off."

"OK, so thank you already," Jessica said. "I'll pay you back first thing tomorrow morning at school. There's only one problem."

"What?" Lila asked.

Jessica giggled. "Do you have change for a hundred?" She didn't actually have a hundred-dollar bill, but Lila didn't have to know that.

"See you tomorrow," Lila said.

Jessica hung up the phone and went into her room. She sat down at her desk and got out her social studies book. She was supposed to read a whole chapter, but she couldn't stop thinking about the money on her dresser. She couldn't wait to get to school and tell the other Unicorns about it!

Instead of taking notes on her reading assignment, Jessica wrote down a list of things she could do with her money.

#1. Clothes.

#2. Compact Discs.

#3. A party for all my friends.

But then she crossed the last one out. The last party she'd had turned into a disaster.

Of course, she *could* pay back some of the money she'd borrowed from Elizabeth. But Elizabeth didn't need it—she had a hundred dollars, too. That could definitely wait.

She took the envelope off her dresser and counted the money again. "I'm rich!" Jessica cried, and that night she dreamed about all she was going to do with her hundred—make that ninety-eight—dollars.

Three

◇

"You're so lucky, Elizabeth," Amy Sutton said the next morning on their way to school. "I'd love it if I had a rich aunt come to visit."

"Aunt Helen's not that rich," Elizabeth said. "That's why we were so surprised. I mean, she's not poor or anything, but she usually gives us ten dollars."

"I wonder why she gave you so much," Amy said.

Elizabeth shrugged. "Maybe one of her stocks paid a lot of money or something. I've heard of that happening before. And she's so nice, she decided to pass the money on to us."

"Who cares how she got it?" Amy asked. "The question is, what are you going to do with it?"

"I don't know yet," Elizabeth said. "I thought

about it a lot last night—I could hardly get my homework done."

"I wish I had those kinds of problems," Amy said.

Elizabeth laughed. "You know how I've been wanting to get a camera. I think maybe I'll save some of the money for that."

"That's a good idea."

"Do you have any suggestions?" Elizabeth asked.

"Well, you could take me to see that new movie at the mall. Or we could go shopping in Los Angeles," Amy said. "Or, you could buy something for Todd."

"Like what?"

"I don't know, you're the one who's going out with him," Amy said. "Get him a new baseball glove or something."

Elizabeth shook her head. "I don't think so."

"OK, then. Let's go to the mall after school today. We can get something to eat, and then we can look around and see if there's anything else you want besides a camera," Amy said.

"Like a few things for you?" Elizabeth joked.

"Well, you might have trouble spending that much money all by yourself," Amy said with a grin.

"I have a feeling it won't be that hard," Elizabeth said, "but you can help me if you want."

Amy put her arm around Elizabeth's shoulder. "Hey, what are best friends for?"

Steven tapped his pencil on his desk. Any minute now, Jill would walk into English class. The first time he saw her every day, he got so nervous he could barely speak. He had never felt so weird around a girl before. He couldn't even remember his own name when Jill was around.

Jill had transferred to Sweet Valley High a few weeks earlier, and she was already one of the most popular girls in the freshman class. She was thin, medium height, and she had blond hair and beautiful green eyes. Steven had fallen for her the first time he saw her.

Just as the bell rang, Jill walked into the room. Steven waved to her. "Hi," he said. "How's it going?" His voice didn't sound quite right—it even squeaked a little.

Jill smiled at him and took her seat in the second row, two seats over from him.

She didn't even say hello, Steven thought dismally. Even though they had hung out together at Casey's the day before, she was acting as if she barely knew him.

That's why I have to ask her out, Steven told himself. And, now that he had a hundred dollars, he was pretty sure that he could impress her. He could even buy her a present. Then she would have to notice him. He could just see Jill's smile when he handed her a big bouquet of roses. Her eyes would light up, and—

"Excuse me, Steven. I don't mean to interrupt your daydream, but would you mind keeping up with the rest of the class?" Mr. Talbert asked.

Steven's head jerked up with a start. "Sorry," he mumbled.

Everyone in the room started snickering, and Steven could feel his face turning red. Out of the corner of his eye, he saw that Jill was laughing, too.

Great, just great, Steven thought. If only Jill knew that he couldn't pay attention in class because he was so busy thinking about her!

"Pass the salt, will you?" Janet Howell said at lunch that day. "This junk has absolutely no taste."

"You're lucky," Jessica said. "Usually it has way too much flavor—bad flavor." She took her sandwich out of a brown paper bag. "I'm glad I brought my own today."

"What do you have?" Janet asked.

"Chicken salad," Jessica said.

"Give me half?" Janet asked. "Please? I'll buy you a dessert."

Jessica handed half of her sandwich down the table to Janet. "It's OK, you don't have to buy me anything." She smiled. "If I want something, I'll get it myself."

Janet looked at her and raised one eyebrow. "I thought you were completely broke."

Jessica didn't really want to tell Janet about her fortune until the rest of the Unicorns sat down at the table. She wanted to make a big announcement in front of everybody. "Well, I was, but I got a little money," Jessica said instead.

"Don't forget to pay Lila back," Janet said. She took a bite of the sandwich.

"I won't." Jessica said. *Why does everyone have to keep bringing that up, anyway?* Jessica thought. It wasn't as if she went around borrowing money and not paying it back all the time. OK, so maybe it had happened once or twice, but it wasn't her fault.

"Hi, you guys!" Mandy Miller sat down at the table. Following her were Kimberly Haver and Ellen Riteman. Every day the Unicorns sat at the same lunch table. They called it the Unicorner. In a minute all of the Unicorns were there, including Lila.

"I'm glad you're all here," Jessica said. "I have a big announcement."

"Are you having another party?" Ellen asked. "Your last one was excellent—until the end, anyway."

Jessica shook her head. "It's better than that. What are you guys doing this afternoon?"

Kimberly shrugged. "Not much. Why?"

"Well, I was thinking of going to the mall," Jessica said. "I thought maybe you'd want to come."

"Why, do you need to borrow more money?" Janet asked. She and Lila laughed.

"No," Jessica said slowly. "I'm going on a major shopping spree!" She looked around the table at everyone and smiled. "I have a hundred dollars—in cash."

"Jessica robbed a bank last night," Lila said.

Jessica sighed. She was sick of Lila's snide comments. "It just so happens that my great-aunt *gave* me a hundred dollars last night, and she said I could spend it all however I wanted to."

"Wow!" Belinda Layton said. "Are you serious?"

Jessica nodded. "That's why I'm going to the mall right after school, to start my shopping spree."

Lila leaned closer and whispered, "You didn't bring it all with you, did you?"

"Sure, why not?" Jessica asked.

"Because!" Lila looked over her shoulder to make sure no one was listening. "You should never carry that much cash. Someone might steal it."

"Don't you think I know that?" Jessica sighed. "Don't worry, I hid the money in a very safe place." Jessica had put the money inside her sock that morning. No one would ever find it there. Her shoe was a little tight, but at least the money was safe.

"Wow, a hundred dollars," Mandy said.

"You can buy a lot of stuff with that," Kimberly added.

"Not really," Lila said. "I mean, it's not really enough for a shopping spree."

"It's not?" Mary asked.

"I could spend a hundred dollars in an hour," Lila said.

"Yeah, but that's because you *practice*," Jessica replied. Mary, Mandy, and Belinda laughed.

"I don't know, I think a hundred is a lot of money," Ellen said. "I've never had that much before. Not all at once, anyway. I don't know what I'd buy first."

"Exactly," Jessica said. "I can't decide what I should do with it. So I was thinking, maybe if you guys come with me—"

"Hey, Jessica," Janet interrupted her. "Remember what you said yesterday? You told Lila that if you had money, you'd spend it on your friends."

"That's right, I did say that." Jessica looked down the table at Lila. "And I'll take everyone

who comes with me out for a sundae at Casey's—
or whatever else you want. You can *even* have a
banana split."

"All right!" Mary cried.

"So, are you coming, Lila?" Jessica asked.

Lila was trying her hardest to look completely
uninterested. "If I don't have anything better to
do," she said.

"I'll pay you back as soon as we get there,"
Jessica said. "It's just that, you know, I have to
get some change—"

"For your hundred," Lila finished for her. "I
know, I know."

Four

◇

"Let's go in here," Elizabeth said, stopping in front of her favorite bookstore in the Valley Mall.

"I should have known we'd end up here," Amy said, following Elizabeth into the store.

"I need a new mystery."

Amy picked up a book. "How about this? *The Case of the Crawling Centipedes?*"

Elizabeth looked at the cover. "I think this is a horror novel, not a mystery," Elizabeth said, making a face. "It would probably give me nightmares."

"I don't know. I think it looks kind of good." Amy opened the book and read the first few lines. "On second thought, never mind. Yuck!" She put it back on the shelf.

Elizabeth began browsing through the mystery section. She liked to read mysteries more than anything else, and she liked one author especially—Amanda Howard. The detective in all of her novels was a woman named Christine Davenport, and Elizabeth thought she was great. Elizabeth had read every single Amanda Howard mystery—all thirty-two of them! Unfortunately, she could read the books a lot faster than Amanda Howard could write them, so she usually found herself waiting for the next one to be published.

"Elizabeth, did you see this?" Amy ran over, holding a copy of *Johnny Buck: The Unauthorized Biography*. Johnny Buck was one of Amy's favorite rock stars. "Look at all these pictures!" Amy flipped through the paperback to the middle section. "Here he is in sixth grade. Can you imagine if *we* had gone to school with Johnny Buck?"

Elizabeth glanced at the photograph. "He looks like he was kind of a nerd."

"He does not," Amy protested. "He was cool. He was just ahead of his time."

"Look at his hair," Elizabeth said. "He must have had a perm then or something."

"OK, so maybe he wasn't perfect." Amy giggled. "He looks like he stuck his finger in an electrical socket!"

Elizabeth started laughing, too. Amy kept

pointing to Johnny Buck's hair and cracking up. Every time Elizabeth heard Amy shriek with laughter, she started laughing even harder.

Finally a sales clerk walked over to them. "May I help you girls with something?"

"Oh, uh, actually, I was looking for a mystery," Elizabeth said. She bit her lip to keep from laughing.

"What do you like to read?" he asked.

"Amanda Howard is my favorite author," Elizabeth replied, "but—"

"She's read everything there is by her," Amy finished.

"Well then, you're in luck!" The clerk led them up toward the front sales counter. "Not only do we have her brand-new book, which just arrived yesterday—"

"You're kidding!" Elizabeth said.

The sales clerk pointed to a big display, and Elizabeth took a copy of the book. "As I was saying, the big news is that Amanda Howard is touring the country to promote her new book. And she'll be here tomorrow afternoon!"

Elizabeth practically dropped the book she was holding. "Tomorrow? Really?"

The sales clerk nodded. "At four o'clock. So, if you buy her book now, you can ask her to sign it tomorrow. Just make sure you bring your receipt."

"That's great, Elizabeth," Amy said.

"I can't believe it," Elizabeth said. "I never thought I'd get to meet her."

"So are you going to buy the book?" Amy asked.

Elizabeth turned the book over in her hands. She didn't usually buy hardcover books. "I don't know. It's twenty-two dollars," she said quietly to Amy.

"So? What's twenty-two dollars?" Amy said. "I mean, you have to spend your money sometime."

Amy does have a point, Elizabeth thought. Aunt Helen had told Elizabeth to buy something she had always wanted with the money. What could be better than an autographed copy of the latest mystery by her favorite writer? "OK, I'll get it," she said, stepping up to the sales counter. Elizabeth took the Johnny Buck biography out of Amy's hands. "And I'll take that, too."

"You don't have to buy that for me," Amy said.

"I know, but I want to," Elizabeth said. She smiled and took out her wallet. She had brought thirty dollars with her. "Besides, whenever we need a good laugh, we can always look at that picture."

"What do you want to do now?" Amy asked after Elizabeth had paid for the book.

"Let's go to Casey's and get a soda," Elizabeth said. "I want to look at the rest of the pictures in your book."

"OK, but if you choke from laughing too hard, it's not my fault," Amy said.

As she and Amy came around the corner and headed down the wing where Casey's was located, Amy suddenly grabbed Elizabeth's arm. "Isn't that Steven, over there in front of that jewelry store?"

Elizabeth looked across the walkway. "You're right, it is him."

"What's he doing at Precious Stones?" Amy asked. "Don't tell me he's going to spend his hundred dollars on a new watch or something boring like that."

"No, I doubt it," Elizabeth said. She thought about the way Steven had watched that girl—Jill— yesterday at Casey's. "I have a funny feeling he's going to buy something for a girl he likes."

"Let's go bug him," Amy said.

"OK, but don't say anything about the girl." She and Amy quietly made their way over toward him, but Steven was so wrapped up in his own thoughts that he didn't even notice when they were right behind him.

"Looking for something?" Amy asked.

Steven jumped and turned around. "What are *you* doing here?"

"Shopping, just like you," Elizabeth said. "So, are you going to buy some jewelry with your hundred dollars?"

"No," Steven said. "I'm, uh, meeting someone here."

"Picking out an engagement ring?" Amy asked. She pointed to a large diamond ring in the display case. "I think that one's pretty nice."

Steven frowned at her. "Don't you have somewhere else to go?"

"Not really," Amy said. She looked up and down the mall walkway. "So who are you meeting?"

"Never mind," Steven said, blushing. "I'll see you later." He took off in the direction of the music store.

Amy and Elizabeth burst out laughing. "He was so nervous!" Elizabeth said. "I've never seen him act so weird about a girl."

"Do you think he was meeting her here?" Amy asked.

Elizabeth shook her head. "He probably wanted to go into the store, only he couldn't, with us here."

Amy laughed. "Can you imagine Steven buying some girl jewelry?"

"If Steven picks it out, I feel sorry for her!" Elizabeth said. "Come on, let's hit Casey's—I'm really thirsty."

"Let's get milkshakes," Amy suggested. They were just about to walk through the door when Jessica walked out, followed by a big group of her friends.

"Hi! What did you buy?" Jessica asked. She peered into the bag her twin was holding.

"It's the latest Amanda Howard mystery," Elizabeth said.

Jessica smiled. "I should have known!"

"Are you telling me you used your hundred dollars to buy a book?" Janet asked.

"What's wrong with that?" Elizabeth replied.

Janet shrugged. "Nothing, it's just not very exciting."

"I think it is," Elizabeth said. "Anyway, the author's going to sign it tomorrow. Did you buy anything yet, Jess?"

"Only sundaes for all my friends." Jessica smiled pointedly at Lila. "We're going to Valley Fashions next."

"Well, see you later," Elizabeth said. "Have fun!" As she watched Jessica walk away, she couldn't help wondering just how much Jessica had spent on their sundaes. There was Kimberly, Grace Oliver, Ellen, Mandy, Mary, Janet, and Lila. That made seven people, plus Jessica had to pay for herself. She had to have spent almost twenty dollars so far.

Then Elizabeth remembered—so had she! In fact, she had spent even more. She had better put some away for her camera. Otherwise it was going to be gone before she knew it. Jessica wasn't the only Wakefield who could spend money!

"Isn't this the coolest bracelet?" Kimberly put a bangle bracelet on her wrist and modeled it for Jessica. "I love it."

"It looks really good with your outfit," Jessica agreed. They were shopping at one of the carts that lined the walkway in the Valley Mall. So far they hadn't made it to Valley Fashions, but Jessica didn't mind. She was having a good time looking at everything. It was fun just knowing she could buy whatever she wanted!

"Check out these earrings," Mary said. She held up a pair of earrings in the shape of carrots.

"Oh, they're you, darling!" Mandy said, laughing.

"Look at these." Lila pointed to a pair of very large silver hoop earrings. "You could practically jump through these!"

"I think they're cool," Jessica said.

"I really want to get this bracelet," Kimberly

said. "Do you think it'll still be here next week? I have to wait for my allowance."

"I know the feeling," Mary said.

"You don't have to wait. I'll get it for you," Jessica offered.

"You will?" Kimberly asked.

"Sure. This is a shopping spree, right? Everyone has to get something, or else it's no fun."

"Are you sure?" Kimberly said. "I mean, it's supposed to be *your* shopping spree."

Jessica looked over at Lila. "What fun is having money if you can't spend it on your friends?" she replied. "Here, let me see that." Kimberly handed her the bracelet and she glanced at the price tag. "It's only four dollars, anyway." Jessica walked over to the cash register, pulling out a five-dollar bill from what was left of the thirty dollars she had transferred from her sock to her pocket before she left school.

"Thank you so much," Kimberly said, slipping it onto her wrist. "You can borrow it any time you want."

"OK, where should we go next?" Jessica asked.

"You guys! Come here!" Ellen called to them from the music store doorway. "You're not going to believe what I found."

Jessica walked over to the store with everyone

else. Music was blaring inside, and the store was packed with kids.

Ellen unrolled a poster from the bin in the front of the store. "It's a poster of Coco!"

"Cool," Grace said. "Look, it has little pictures around the edges from her concert."

"And lyrics, too," Mary pointed out.

"Isn't this a great picture of her?" Ellen asked. "I would love to have this in my bedroom."

"How much is it?" Jessica asked.

Ellen found the price sticker on the poster wrapper. "Five dollars," she said. "That's not bad." She slipped the poster back into its plastic wrapper and put it back in the bin.

"Don't you want it?" Jessica asked.

"Yeah, but I only have two dollars on me," Ellen said. "I guess I'll come back."

"They'll be all gone by then," Jessica predicted. She took three dollars out of her pocket and handed them to Ellen. "You'd better get it now."

"Really?" Ellen asked. "OK, I'll pay you back after my next baby-sitting job. I think I'm sitting for the Parsons this weekend."

Jessica shook her head. "Don't bother." She wasn't going to demand that her friends pay her back the way Lila did.

"Jessica, this shopping spree was a really good idea," Ellen said when they left the music store. "I can't wait to put up my new poster. You'll have to come over and see it."

"Hey, Jessica, you can't go home without buying something for yourself," Mary said. "Want to hit Valley Fashions now?"

"OK," Jessica said.

They were halfway there when Grace stopped at another cart. "These hair ribbons are beautiful!" She held the thin gold and blue striped ribbon against her dark brown hair. "What do you think, Jessica?"

"They're perfect. You could weave them into a braid," Jessica said.

In another minute, everyone was gathered around the cart, trying out various hair accessories. Jessica had a feeling she wouldn't make it to her favorite clothing store that afternoon. But she didn't care—she still had almost seventy dollars. She could come back the next day. And best of all, what made her feel great was that she had shown Lila it was possible to be rich *and* generous!

Steven glanced at his watch. It was almost five o'clock. Jessica and Elizabeth usually went home around then, so maybe it would be safe for him to go back out into the mall. He had been hanging out at the snack bar in a cheap department store for an hour, drinking soda after soda, waiting for them to disappear. Sometimes he wished he lived in a big city like Los Angeles, so he wouldn't run into his younger sisters all the time.

Steven paid the check and walked out into the mall. He quickly made his way back toward Precious Stones. With a quick glance over his shoulder, Steven ducked into the jewelry store.

A salesman wearing a suit looked at him suspiciously from behind the counter. "May I help you?"

Steven cleared his throat. "Yes, I'm, uh, interested in some of the earrings you have in the window."

The man walked around the counter, peering at Steven's ears. "What kind do you like?"

Steven felt himself blush. "They're not for me, they're for my, uh, girlfriend." *Wishful thinking,* he added in his head. He pointed to a pair of diamond earrings in the window. He could just picture how good they would look next to Jill's shiny blond hair. "How much are those?" he asked.

The salesman unlocked the case and took out the earrings. "Beautiful, aren't they? You can't go wrong with diamonds. And this week we're having a sale on all of our fine jewelry. These are only three hundred and seventy dollars." He handed the earring box to Steven and smiled.

"Is that before you mark them down?" Steven asked.

"After," the man said. "So, shall I wrap them for you?"

"Well, uh, that's a little out of my price range," Steven said, handing the velvet box back to the salesman.

"What exactly is your price range?" the salesman asked.

"I'm not sure," Steven said. "I mean, I have a lot of money, but I don't want to spend it all on earrings. Not that earrings are a bad thing to spend money on," he added quickly, when he saw the salesman's expression. "It's just that, you know, we'll be going out to dinner and everything too."

"Special occasion?" the salesman asked.

"Kind of," Steven answered.

"How about something a little less extravagant then." The salesman took out a pair of gold, dangling earrings with pearls. "These are only two hundred."

"Less extravagant than that," Steven said.

"All right." The salesman picked up some earrings with green stones. "These are seventy-five."

Steven was tempted. The green stones were exactly the same color as Jill's eyes. But if he bought them, the only place he could afford to take her would be the Dairi Burger. Besides, she might think he was weird if he gave her some really fancy earrings. And now that he thought about it, Steven wasn't sure if Jill had pierced ears. She did . . . didn't she?

"Well?" the salesman prompted.

"I think they're too fancy," Steven said.

"How about some plain gold posts then?" Steven followed the salesman up to the counter. "These are twenty-eight dollars, they're real gold, and they go with everything. Girls love them. Trust me."

Steven looked at the earrings. They were kind of small. Would anyone even be able to see them if Jill wore them? They reminded him of something that his mother would wear. Still, they were real gold.

"Young man, if you want something less extravagant than these, you're going to have to try the five-and-dime across the mall," the salesman said impatiently.

"OK, I'll take them," Steven said.

"Fine," the salesman said.

Steven watched him put them in a black box with the Precious Stones logo on it. At least Jill would know that he bought them at an expensive store. The salesman wrapped the box in shiny gold paper and tied a black ribbon around it. He couldn't wait to see Jill's face when she opened the box—she was going to be so impressed.

"What's your returns policy?" Steven asked, just in case Jill wasn't impressed.

"Pierced earrings can't be returned," the salesman said. "But don't worry—she'll love them."

Five

◇

"So, what did you three do after school?" Mrs. Wakefield asked when the family sat down to dinner that night.

Mr. Wakefield smiled and handed a plate of roast beef to her. "I'm surprised you need to ask."

"We went to the mall," Jessica said, helping herself to scalloped potatoes.

"That sounds like fun," Aunt Helen said. "Did you get anything?"

"Not for me," Jessica said. "I treated my friends to sundaes at Casey's, though."

"How thoughtful!" Aunt Helen exclaimed. She took a sip of water. "What about you, Elizabeth?"

"I went to the bookstore, and it turned out that my favorite writer in the whole world just came out with a new book. And I found out that she's coming to Sweet Valley tomorrow for a book signing!"

"Amanda Howard?" Mrs. Wakefield asked.

Elizabeth nodded. "I'm going back tomorrow to have her autograph my book. Isn't that exciting?"

"It certainly is," Aunt Helen said. "You know, I've read some of her books."

"Elizabeth's read *all* of them," Jessica said.

"Would you like to come to the bookstore with me tomorrow?" Elizabeth asked Aunt Helen.

"No, I don't think so," Aunt Helen said. "I'd like to meet her, but I don't feel quite up to being in the middle of a big crowd."

"Someone might bump your cast, you mean?" Jessica said.

"Yes," Aunt Helen said.

"I guess it will be pretty crowded," Elizabeth said. "I'd better get there early."

"Too bad you don't have your camera yet," Jessica said. "You could get a picture of you and her together."

"You're right. I hadn't thought of that," Elizabeth said. "I guess her signature will be good enough."

"Steven? What about you? You've hardly said a word," Aunt Helen observed.

"I'm OK," Steven said. He chewed and stared straight ahead.

"You look like you're in a trance," Jessica said.

"Maybe he's thinking about how he's going to spend his money," Mr. Wakefield said.

"Sort of," Steven said, still staring into space.

"Well, I'm glad you're all enjoying it," Aunt Helen said. "Jessica, could you pass the potatoes?"

"Sure thing." Jessica handed the dish to her great-aunt. "Do you want me to serve them for you? I could cut your roast beef for you, too."

Aunt Helen laughed. "No thank you. I'm not completely helpless, you know!"

"How long did the doctor say you'd be stuck wearing that cast?" Mr. Wakefield asked.

"Six weeks or so," Aunt Helen replied. "I wish I didn't have to wear it. I feel like a mummy."

"But you can't be a mummy," Steven said. "You're a great-aunt!"

Jessica groaned. "Why don't you go back to your trance? That was the worst joke you've ever told!"

"How did you break your arm again?" Elizabeth asked.

"Oh, I was just clumsy," Aunt Helen answered.

"Were you at home when it happened?" Jessica asked.

Aunt Helen sat back in her chair and dabbed

her mouth with a napkin. "You know, those are the best scalloped potatoes I have ever tasted. In fact, everything tastes delicious."

"Thank you," Mrs. Wakefield said.

"What about me?" Mr. Wakefield asked. He winked at Aunt Helen. "I sliced the roast."

"Nice slices, Dad," Jessica said, rolling her eyes. "You should be a chef instead of a lawyer."

"Or at least work in a deli," Mrs. Wakefield said, laughing.

Jessica knocked on Steven's door after dinner. "OK if I come in?"

"No," Steven replied. "Just a second."

Jessica pressed her ear against the door. She could hear him putting something away in his desk.

"OK, come in if you have to," Steven said a moment later.

"What are you doing?" Jessica asked, coming into the room.

Steven turned around in his desk chair. "I was about to do my homework. Why?"

"I was just wondering." Jessica pushed some of Steven's clothes onto the floor to make room for her to sit down on his bed. "So, what are you going to do with your money?"

Steven shrugged. "I don't know. Why, do you want to borrow it?"

"Ha ha." Jessica picked up a baseball cap from the floor and put it on her head. "It's just—"

"Hi." Elizabeth poked her head in the doorway.

"I'm trying to find out how Steven's going to spend his money," Jessica said. "Only he's not telling."

"I didn't say I wouldn't tell you. I'll probably get some CDs, you know, maybe a new basketball." Steven tossed a crumpled piece of paper across the room, and it landed in his wastebasket.

Elizabeth walked into the room. "Is that all?"

"Sure. What else would I get?"

"Oh, I don't know . . ." Elizabeth tapped her chin. "Expensive jewelry?"

Jessica burst out laughing. "Yeah, right!"

"I saw him standing outside Precious Stones today," Elizabeth said.

Steven's face turned red. "I'm not buying any jewelry. I told you, I was meeting somebody there."

Jessica watched her brother carefully. She had a feeling he wasn't telling them the whole story.

"You weren't buying a present for somebody?" Elizabeth asked.

"Well, while I was standing there, I did kind of think about getting something nice for Mom or Aunt Helen," Steven said, doodling in his notebook.

"Now I *know* you're lying," Jessica said.

"Wait—I know! I bet you were buying something for that girl we saw you with yesterday at Casey's."

"You were at Casey's yesterday?" Steven asked.

"Yeah, only you didn't see us because you were in a trance, just like tonight at dinner," Jessica said. "Face it, Steven, you're definitely in love with this girl."

Elizabeth nodded. "Definitely."

"I am not!" Steven said. "Anyway, I don't even know who you're taking about."

"Sure you don't," Elizabeth said, skeptically. "She has blond hair about to here—" Elizabeth held her hand just above her shoulder. "She's really pretty."

"You think so?" Steven asked in a squeaky voice. He cleared his throat. "I mean, you must be talking about Jill Hale."

"So what did you buy her?" Jessica asked. "A necklace? A bracelet? What?"

"I didn't buy her anything," Steven said. "Why would I?"

"Come *on*, Steven, you can tell us," Elizabeth said. "You really like her, right?"

Steven shrugged. "She's OK."

Jessica looked at Elizabeth and rolled her eyes.

"Well, if I were you, and I had a hundred

dollars and I really liked a girl, I'd take her out on an extra-special date," Jessica said.

Steven kept doodling in his notebook, but Jessica could tell he was listening to her.

"You could take her to some really fancy restaurant and buy her flowers," Jessica continued. "Of course, jewelry would be nice, too. You could give it to her on your date. Then she'd definitely fall for you."

"Jessica, he doesn't have to do all that for her to like him," Elizabeth said.

"No, but it wouldn't hurt," Jessica said.

"Are you done yet?" Steven said, glaring at Jessica.

"I'm just trying to help," Jessica said, standing up. "But since you're not interested in this girl at all, I might as well forget it." She turned to go.

"Yeah, that must have been someone else we saw at Casey's, staring at her," Elizabeth said.

The twins ducked just in time to miss the notebook Steven threw at them.

Elizabeth put down her new book, *Stolen Evidence*, and rubbed her eyes. She had been reading for an hour and a half straight, ever since she finished her homework. She wanted to finish the book before she met Amanda Howard, so she could talk to her about it. Besides, Elizabeth couldn't wait to find out who the murderer was!

She looked at the clock. It was almost nine thirty. There was no way she could finish it that night, but if she read a little while longer, she might be able to solve the crime. She decided to go downstairs and get a glass of juice.

In the kitchen, Elizabeth poured herself some juice and wandered into the living room. She thought Aunt Helen might be watching TV, but she was already in her room, the den. The light was shining out from underneath the door.

Elizabeth was about to knock on the door when she heard her great-aunt's voice. "What am I going to do if I have to go to court?" she said.

Then Elizabeth heard another voice—her father's.

"Don't worry, Helen, we'll make sure you get a good lawyer," Mr. Wakefield said. "If one of the people I've recommended can't help you, I'll fly out there and help you myself."

Why would Aunt Helen need a lawyer? Elizabeth wondered.

"After all, you need someone to protect you from those sharks," Mr. Wakefield went on.

"They can be very unpleasant," Aunt Helen said. "You should have heard the way they talked to me before I left!"

"Well, don't let them bully you," Mr. Wakefield said.

Elizabeth wasn't sure what they were talking about, but it didn't sound good. She wanted to go in and find out what was going on, but if she did, they would know she had been eavesdropping. They probably wouldn't be very happy about that.

What sharks was her father talking about? And who was bullying Aunt Helen?

Maybe she's in trouble! Elizabeth thought. But that was ridiculous—Aunt Helen was visiting them just like she always did. She had a broken arm, but that was just an accident.

Or was it? Elizabeth wondered as she went back upstairs.

Then she shook her head. *I'm so wrapped up in my mystery I'm turning everything into a mystery!*

Steven stared at the words in his notebook. He had been trying to memorize them for the past half hour. He said them again, just to make sure he wouldn't mess up.

"Hi, Jill, this is Steven. How are you? I was wondering if you'd like to go out with me this Friday night. I thought maybe we could go to dinner, say, around seven. How does that sound?"

"That sounds like you're a total dweeb!" Steven answered himself. He chewed his thumbnail. He'd been fiddling with his speech all night, trying to make it come out right. It wasn't that he hadn't asked a girl out before. He'd just never asked Jill out before. He'd never even talked to her on the phone.

Well, it's now or never, Steven told himself, taking a deep breath. On the way to the hall phone, he tripped over a magazine that someone had slipped under his door. Steven leaned over to pick it up. The magazine was open to an article called, "My Dream Date." On it there was a sticker saying, "Read This!" It looked like Jessica's handwriting.

As dumb as it looked, Steven couldn't help skimming the article. It was written by a teenage girl, and it was all about how some boy had taken her out on this incredibly fantastic date. He had given her flowers and a gift; they had gone out to dinner at a fancy restaurant; then they had gone dancing . . .

"Dancing?" Steven said out loud. He wasn't so sure about that. But according to this article, his plans for a perfect evening weren't totally off base. If the girl who had written this article had liked it enough to call it a "dream date," wouldn't Jill?

Steven brought the phone into his room and closed the door. He didn't even need to glance at

Jill's phone number in his notebook. He had traced it so many times, he'd worn a hole in the page.

"Hello?" a woman's voice answered.

"Hello," Steven said. "Is Jill there?"

"This is Jill," she said. "Who's this?"

Steven couldn't believe it—he hadn't even recognized her voice! "It's Steven," he said. When she didn't respond, he said, "Steven Wakefield."

"Oh, hi, Steven," Jill said. "What's up?"

"Not much. Just working on my English homework." Steven laughed nervously.

"We didn't have any," Jill reminded him.

"Right," Steven said. "That was a joke."

"Oh," Jill said.

Steven fumbled for his script. So far things weren't going the way he'd planned. "I was wondering if you'd like to go out with me Friday night," he mumbled.

"Sorry. What was that about Friday?" Jill asked.

"Uh, are you doing anything?" Steven asked.

"Probably," Jill said. "I don't know what yet."

"Well, would you like to go out?" Steven asked. "To dinner?"

Jill didn't answer right away, and for a second Steven was afraid she had hung up. "I guess that would be OK," she finally said.

Steven heaved a sigh of relief. "Great!"

"Where are we going?" Jill asked.

"I'm not sure yet," Steven said. "It'll be a surprise, OK?"

"Sure, as long as it's not the Valley Diner," Jill said.

Steven laughed. "Don't worry, it'll be a lot better than that."

"I have to go. My mom won't let me talk to anyone after ten," Jill said.

"OK. I'll see you tomorrow," Steven said. "Don't forget about Friday night."

"I won't. Good night." Jill hung up the phone.

For a minute Steven just sat on his bed, too stunned to move. He actually had a date with Jill Hale.

Then he panicked. What if she thought Steven Wakefield was someone else? There were a lot of guys named Steven at school. She could have confused him with some other guy.

Then he remembered that he had mentioned English class, so she had to know it was him. "Yes!" Steven whispered, throwing his fist in the air. He and Jill had a date—and it was less than two days away!

Six

◇

Elizabeth took a little extra time getting ready on Thursday morning. She wanted to look nice when she met Amanda Howard. It wasn't every day that she got to talk with her favorite author!

"You look nice today," Mrs. Wakefield said when Elizabeth went downstairs for breakfast.

"Thanks," Elizabeth said. "Remember this sweater, Aunt Helen? You gave it to me last year for Christmas."

Aunt Helen smiled. "I thought it looked familiar."

"Are you sure you don't want to meet me at the mall for the book signing?" Elizabeth asked.

"I could take you over there, Helen," Mrs. Wakefield offered.

Aunt Helen set down her coffee mug. "No,

thank you," she said. "I'm enjoying being a hermit."

"It's unusual for you not to run around and do things," Mr. Wakefield said. "Last year you almost replanted our entire garden."

"I planted a few flowers," Aunt Helen said, laughing. "Anyway, I had use of both my arms then."

"True," Mr. Wakefield said. "But don't worry, I'm sure it'll heal soon."

Just then, Jessica appeared in the kitchen and took a seat at the table. Steven followed a minute later, looking extremely tired.

"You look terrible," Jessica commented.

"Thanks," Steven said, his voice practically croaking. He took a sip of grapefruit juice and grimaced.

"Were you up late studying last night?" Mr. Wakefield asked.

"No," Steven said. "I just couldn't fall asleep, that's all."

"What's the matter? Is there something on your mind?" Aunt Helen asked.

Jessica snickered and poked Elizabeth in the leg.

Steven glared at her. "Not really. Anyway, what's for breakfast?"

"Cereal, toast, the usual," Mr. Wakefield said. "Help yourself."

The doorbell rang just as Steven was reaching for the milk. He was so surprised, he almost spilled it all over himself.

"Who could that be?" Mrs. Wakefield wondered. "It's not even eight o'clock."

Elizabeth jumped up. "I'll get it."

A woman in a blue and red uniform was standing on the steps. "Good morning," she said. "Is this the Wakefield residence?"

Elizabeth nodded.

"I'm with Overnight Delivery Service. I have a package here for a Helen Robertson." The woman held out a clipboard and a pen. "Sign on line seven, please."

Elizabeth signed the sheet of paper, and the messenger handed her a large flat envelope. "Thank you," she said.

"Have a nice day!" the messenger called. She got into her van and backed out of the driveway.

Elizabeth examined the envelope and brought it to Aunt Helen.

"What is it?" Jessica asked.

"Maybe Aunt Helen won the sweepstakes," Steven said.

"I don't think so," Aunt Helen said with a smile. She set it on the windowsill beside her.

"Aren't you going to open it?" Elizabeth asked.

"I know what it is," Aunt Helen said. "It's not important."

"Then why did they rush it to you?" Steven asked.

"They just wanted to make sure it was delivered, that's all," Aunt Helen said.

"Who's they?" Elizabeth asked.

"Aren't you dying of curiosity?" Jessica said. "Come on, open it."

"Don't badger Aunt Helen," Mr. Wakefield said. "She'll open it when she wants to. Besides, it's nothing exciting."

"It isn't?" Jessica asked.

"No," Aunt Helen said. "Believe me, it's nothing. It's just some business I have to take care of when I get home."

Elizabeth looked at her great-aunt. She wondered if this business had anything to do with what Aunt Helen and her father had been discussing the night before. Maybe the letter was from her lawyer. Why wouldn't Aunt Helen tell them what it was? Especially since she said it was "nothing."

"Come on, it's time you three left for school," Mrs. Wakefield said.

Elizabeth got up slowly. She didn't know whether she was imagining things or not, but it seemed as if Aunt Helen was nervous. She kept fingering the package, and she looked worried.

"I hope you get to meet Amanda Howard today," Mr. Wakefield said.

"Me, too," Elizabeth said, checking to make sure she'd put the new book in her knapsack. But she was most concerned about the mystery that seemed to be brewing right here at home.

"I'm so glad you came with me," Elizabeth told Amy as they walked into the mall that afternoon after school. "I'm kind of nervous about meeting *the* Amanda Howard."

"Don't worry," Amy said. "I bet she's really nice."

"I'm just afraid I'll do something really dumb, like drop my book on her toes," Elizabeth admitted.

Amy laughed. "You'll be fine," she said. "Hey. Can you sleep over on Friday? We can rent a movie and stay up to watch that new TV show, 'Staying Up With Bob.' "

"Sure that sounds fun," Elizabeth said. "I have to check with—Amy! It's her!" Elizabeth hurried into the bookstore. Amanda Howard was sitting at a table up front, and there was a line of about twenty people waiting to have her autograph.

"It's a good thing we got here early," Amy said as they got in line. She pointed at the pyramid of books stacked on the table next to Amanda

Howard. "Do you really think they'll sell all those?"

"Sure. She's really popular." Elizabeth stepped out of the line to get a better look at Amanda. She looked the same as she did on her book jackets. "I can't believe she's actually here in the bookstore where I buy all her books," Elizabeth said.

"It's pretty cool," Amy said. "What are you going to ask her?"

"I'd like to talk to her about writing," Elizabeth said. "But I don't think she has time. I think I'll just ask her to sign this." She took her copy of *Stolen Evidence* out of her knapsack.

They only had to wait ten minutes, but it felt like an hour to Elizabeth. When Amanda Howard finally looked up and smiled at her, Elizabeth thought she was going to pass out.

"How shall I sign it?" Amanda asked.

"To Elizabeth," she said.

"My biggest fan," Amy added.

"No, you don't have to write that," Elizabeth said. "Just 'to Elizabeth' is fine."

Amanda looked up at her and smiled. "Are you really a big fan?"

"Yes," Elizabeth said. "I've read every single one of your books—well, except this one. I'm almost done, though. I didn't get it until yesterday."

"Do you like it so far?" Amanda asked.

Elizabeth nodded eagerly. "I can't wait to see what's going to happen to the gardener."

Amanda smiled. "I couldn't either!" She signed the first page of the book with a fountain pen. Her handwriting was neat, and Elizabeth could read every word even before Amanda handed the book back to her.

"To Elizabeth," it said. "I'm glad someone knows how to pick out the important details in a mystery! If you keep reading, I'll keep writing. Best of luck, Amanda Howard."

"Thank you so much!" Elizabeth said. "Can I ask you one question, before we go?"

"Sure," Amanda said.

"How do you come up with the ideas for your books? I mean, you've written so many," Elizabeth said. "How did you think of all those plots?"

"Elizabeth's a writer, too," Amy said, "so she needs to know this kind of thing."

"Well, it's simple, really," Amanda said. "Most of the time, there are mysteries going on right under our noses. We just don't notice them. I pay attention, that's all."

"Well, I guess we have to go," Elizabeth said. "Thanks for signing my book—I mean, your book. I hope you'll come back when you finish the next one."

"I'll try!" Amanda Howard waved to Elizabeth and Amy with her pen, then turned to sign the next customer's book.

"She was *so* nice," Amy said once they were outside the store.

"I know." Elizabeth looked back at her. "I almost feel like buying another book and waiting in line just so I can talk to her again."

"Yeah, but look at how long the line is," Amy said.

Elizabeth opened the book and reread what Amanda had written. "This is great," she said.

"Yeah," Amy said, then sighed. "I wonder when Johnny Buck is going to come here and sign *my* book!"

"OK, five small cones—that comes to six eighty-seven." The boy working at the frozen yogurt stand in the food court held out his hand.

Jessica reached into her pockets. "Whoops," she muttered. "Just a second."

"Don't tell me you ran out of money already," Lila said.

"Are you kidding? Here, hold this for a second." Jessica handed Lila her cone, then leaned down and felt inside her sock for her wad of money. She pulled it out and unrolled a ten-dollar bill, which she handed to the boy.

He held it a few feet away from him and wrinkled his nose, as if the money smelled. Lila and everyone else in their group cracked up. The boy slid it into the cash register and got out Jessica's change. "Here's your change. If you want, you can just hand me your shoe and I'll put it in."

"No thanks," Jessica said, blushing. She took the change and put it in the pocket of her jeans. Lila handed her the cone, and they went back out into the mall.

"He was cute, don't you think?" Tamara Chase asked.

"What a wise guy," Jessica muttered.

"Come on, he was just teasing you," Janet said. "I thought I was going to die when you handed him that money from your sock!"

"When you said your money was in a safe place, I had no idea," Lila said. "Haven't you ever heard of a bank?"

"You can't put your money in a bank when you're going shopping," Jessica said. She licked her blueberry frozen yogurt.

"Thanks for the yogurt," Mandy said. "This is really good."

"Yeah, you didn't have to buy it for all of us," Tamara said.

"No problem," Jessica said.

"Tamara's right, you know," Lila said. "You shouldn't keep buying ice cream for everyone."

"Why not?" Jessica took a bite of her cone.

"Because you're not going to have any money left," Lila said.

"I have plenty left. Anyway, you're only saying that because you're jealous," Jessica said.

"Jealous of what?" Lila scoffed.

"The fact that I have more money than you, for once," Jessica said. "And the fact that I'm generous enough to spend it on my friends."

Lila tossed her napkin into a trash can. "Well, if you're not careful, you could be dead broke again tomorrow."

"Just because you hog all your money doesn't mean I have to," Jessica said. "My aunt told me to enjoy it, so I am. I like buying things for other people."

"I'm just trying to give you some good advice," Lila said. "I know what I'm talking about. No one will remember that you bought them stuff."

Jessica stopped in front of Valley Fashions and finished her yogurt. "I want to go in here for a few minutes, OK?" she asked when everyone had caught up.

"Sure," Belinda said, "whatever you want."

Jessica walked over to a shirt that was hanging on the "new arrivals" rack. "Isn't this cool?" she asked. It was a short-sleeved blouse with swirls of bright colors all over it. She turned over the price tag.

"How much is it?" Lila asked.

"Thirty-nine ninety-nine," Jessica said.

"You should get it," Tamara said. "Try it on, anyway."

Jessica held the blouse up to her. The material was really nice, and she had never seen anyone wearing a pattern quite like it—not at Sweet Valley Middle School, anyway. But she wasn't sure if she wanted to spend forty dollars right away. If she did, she'd hardly be left with any money— and Lila would be right. Besides, she wanted to make sure there wasn't something else she wanted more than the shirt before she went ahead and bought it. Jessica sighed. When Jessica was broke, which she usually was, she had no trouble spending forty dollars. But now that she had all this money, she couldn't make up her mind to buy anything.

Jessica slipped it back onto the rack. "I think I'll wait."

"I can't believe it," Lila pretended to look shocked. "There's actually something you're not going to buy?"

"Hey, Jessica, while you're thinking it over, can I show you a T-shirt I want to get?" Tamara asked.

"Sure," Jessica said.

"It's at one of those little booths in the middle of the mall. Actually, it's not there *now*, because they haven't made it yet. They spray paint your name on it while you watch!"

"I've seen those before," Jessica said. "How much are they?"

"They're usually ten dollars," Tamara said, "but the guy told me they're on sale this week—they're only *six* dollars. Come on, I'll show you."

Lila shook her head as Jessica linked her arm through Tamara's. "Let's go!" Jessica said happily.

Seven

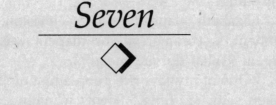

"Amy, do you hear that?" Elizabeth asked. The girls were sitting in the Wakefields' kitchen drinking juice later that afternoon.

"Hear what?" Amy asked.

"Shh," Elizabeth said. The more she listened, the more it sounded as if someone were crying. She tiptoed through the hall into the living room. There, sitting on the couch, was Aunt Helen—and she was sobbing!

"Aunt Helen, what's wrong?" Elizabeth asked rushing over to her.

Aunt Helen wiped her eyes and cleared her throat. "Oh, Elizabeth, I didn't even hear you come in."

"We just got back from the mall," Elizabeth said. She touched Aunt Helen's shoulder. "What's wrong? Are you OK?" All of a sudden the words she had heard last night came back to her: *Don't let them bully you*, her father had said. Was somebody trying to hurt Aunt Helen?

Aunt Helen pointed at the television. "It's embarrassing, really. I was crying because of that silly thing."

Elizabeth glanced at the television. At the moment, a commercial for diapers was on the screen. "What do you mean?"

"One of my favorite people just died," Aunt Helen said, sniffling. "I was watching 'Days of Turmoil.' You know, I've been watching it for almost twenty years now. Ever since I started watching it, there's been this nurse, Mary Lloyd."

Elizabeth nodded.

"She's always been my favorite character," Aunt Helen explained. "A few weeks ago she got to be friends with a dangerous patient—of course, she didn't know he was dangerous. It turned out he came from a family of gangsters, and the reason he was in the hospital was that someone had attempted to take his life."

"So what happened to the nurse?" Elizabeth asked.

"Well, she was in the hospital room, about to give this man his medication, when a man from *another* gangster family came in to try to kill him again." Aunt Helen paused and dabbed her eyes with a tissue. "Since Nurse Lloyd was in the room, he had to kill her, too."

"He shot her?" Elizabeth said. "Right there in the hospital?"

Aunt Helen nodded.

"Maybe she's not really dead," Elizabeth said hopefully. "You know how they always bring people back on soap operas. She's probably just pretending to be dead."

Aunt Helen shook her head. "I don't think so. Today was her funeral."

"Oh." Elizabeth looked at her shoes. In a way she was glad Aunt Helen had only been crying about "Days of Turmoil." *At least I hope that's all it is*, Elizabeth thought.

"Jessica watches 'Days of Turmoil,' too," Elizabeth said. "She's always talking about it."

"I'll have to break the news to her then," Aunt Helen said.

For some reason, Elizabeth had trouble believing that Aunt Helen—reasonable, dependable, witty Aunt Helen—could get so concerned about a soap opera character. It didn't make sense. And there was something else she was curious about, too. "Aunt Helen, did you open that letter you got?" she asked.

"What letter?" Aunt Helen replied.

"You know, the one they specially delivered this morning," Elizabeth said. *Aunt Helen had only gotten* one *letter while she was staying with them*, Elizabeth thought suspiciously.

"Oh, yes, I did. It was just as I thought— nothing interesting," Aunt Helen said. "Now, tell me, did you get to talk to Amanda Howard?"

"Yeah, it was great," Elizabeth said.

A few minutes later, Elizabeth went back to the kitchen for Amy and motioned for her to follow her up to her room. Once they were inside her bedroom, Elizabeth shut the door.

"What's the big secret?" Amy asked, sitting down on the bed.

"That's what *I* want to know." Elizabeth set her glass down on the desk and started pacing back and forth. "Something weird is going on." Elizabeth explained to Amy all about her Aunt Helen and the soap opera. "And this morning she got this letter," Elizabeth said. "It was a big deal, you know, an overnight delivery thing, but she wouldn't tell us what it was."

"Maybe it's private," Amy said. "Maybe she's thinking about giving you *more* money!"

"I don't think so. I wouldn't have thought the letter was was so strange except that last night I heard her talking to my father about how she might have to go to court. She said someone had been bullying her, or something like that," Elizabeth explained.

"Really?" Amy asked. "But why?"

Elizabeth shrugged. "Beats me. Maybe I'm making something out of nothing, but it seems like whenever I ask Aunt Helen about stuff, she says it's nothing. Like that letter. Why doesn't she just tell me who it's from?"

"Maybe the letter was a threat or something," Amy suggested. "You know how people cut letters from magazines and send notes to people?"

"You mean like a ransom note?" Elizabeth asked.

"Right! It could be a ransom note," Amy said excitedly.

"For what, though? That doesn't make sense," Elizabeth said.

"Hm." Amy sipped her orange juice. "Has she done anything else weird?"

"Well, she's staying inside a lot more than she usually does, but I guess that's just because of her broken arm."

"How did she break it?" Amy asked.

"I'm not sure exactly. She didn't say how it happened."

"Elizabeth!" Amy exclaimed, jumping up from the bed. "Your aunt is in big trouble! Someone's after her!"

"Do you really think so?" Elizabeth asked.

"I bet the same guys who sent her that threatening letter broke her arm," Amy said.

"We don't know that it was a threat," Elizabeth said. Still, even though Amy tended to jump to conclusions, everything had to be connected somehow. But why in the world would someone be after Aunt Helen?

She remembered what Amanda Howard had told her that afternoon: "Most of the time, there are mysteries going on right under our noses."

"I don't know what to do," she told Amy. "I don't want to bring it up if it's going to upset her. But I want to find out if there really is something bad going on."

"There's only one thing to do," Amy said. "We have to get our hands on that letter."

Steven knew he should be heading home for dinner, but there was no way he was going to leave the Dairi Burger. He was sitting next to Jill, and he wasn't going to move until she did.

Of course, there were five other people at the table, but Steven didn't care.

"Larry, did you plug in that shirt or what?" Joe Howell asked. He held up his hands and pretended to shield himself from the light. "Talk about neon!"

Larry Harris grinned and brushed off his neon orange T-shirt. "Hey, look at it this way, at least I won't get hit by a car."

"No kidding," Joe said. "A plane could see you from thirty thousand feet."

Jill threw back her head and laughed. She was leaning forward in the booth, and her blond hair swayed in front of Steven's face."

"Oh, and your clothes are a lot better," Larry said.

"What can I say?" Joe stood up and turned around, pretending to be a model. He was wearing white jeans, a striped blue and white shirt, and deck shoes.

"You look like the skipper on a cruise ship," Steven said. "Welcome aboard the SS *Howell*," he added and saluted Joe. Cathy Connors, Megan Moore, and Larry all cracked up. Steven looked eagerly at Jill for her reaction. She was gazing at Joe.

"Hey, wasn't that the name of the millionaire on 'Gilligan's Island'?" Cathy said.

"That's right, Mr. Howell!" Steven said. "Gilligan's Island is definitely where Joe's ship would end up," Steven said. Joe was one of his best friends, but they made fun of each other all the time.

"Wakefield, do I have to remind you of the

time you said you knew a shortcut to school—and we ended up three miles outside of town?" Joe said, sitting back down at the end of the booth.

Jill started laughing. "No, really?"

"Yeah, it was about two years ago. We were late because we'd been horsing around on our bikes, so Steven said he knew this new way to go. Half an hour later, we see this sign: Welcome to Big Mesa!" Joe laughed. "Remember how mad Mr. Clark got?"

"Didn't you get detention?" Cathy said.

Steven nodded. "For a week. I don't know why he was so mad. We were only an hour and a half late."

Jill turned to face Steven, and he felt his heart start to beat faster. "How could you get lost around here?" she asked. "This is the smallest town I've ever lived in."

Now she thinks I'm an idiot, Steven thought. "I don't know, I guess I just got mixed up."

"It was too early in the morning," Joe said. "Not a lot of people know this, but Steven doesn't turn into a human until nine o'clock."

Cathy and Megan laughed. "Yeah, if you've ever had a first period class with him, you'd know that," Cathy said.

Jill didn't seem to care whether she had *any* classes with Steven. Was she dreading their date the next night? He obviously wasn't making a very good impression.

Joe went up to the counter to get another soda. *Here's my chance*, Steven decided. "So, Jill," he said. "Where are you from? I mean, where did you live before you came here—to Sweet Valley, I mean."

"Different places," Jill said. "My dad keeps getting transferred because he's a computer expert. He works for a really big company, and they send him to different offices all the time."

"Have you ever loved—I mean lived—in Europe?" Steven wanted to kick himself. He hoped no one else had heard that.

But no one seemed to have noticed—least of all Jill. "Yeah, we lived in France for a while," she said.

"That must have been neat," Steven said. *Listen to me—neat? That's something Aunt Helen would say!*

Joe came back to the table, carrying a soda and a box of French fries. "These are for you, Jill," he said, sliding the box in front of her. "You looked hungry."

"Thanks!" Jill said. She picked up a fry and popped it in her mouth.

"Hey, no fair," Cathy complained. "What about the rest of us?"

"Didn't I just see you eat a cheeseburger with the works?" Joe said.

"No, that wasn't me," Cathy said innocently.

Everyone laughed, except Steven. He felt like he couldn't do anything right where Jill was concerned. He could just as easily have gotten her a box of fries, but it hadn't occurred to him. "Do you want some ketchup?" he asked Jill.

"Sure," she said.

"I'll get it," Joe said.

"No, I'll get it," Steven said, standing up quickly. "I want to, uh, get some fries, too."

"Get a lot," Megan said.

Steven ordered an extra large basket of fries and grabbed a bunch of ketchup packets from the bowl on the counter. When he went back to the table, he put the fries in the middle and said, "Help yourselves!" At least Jill would see that he was generous. Anyway, so what if Joe bought her a little box of greasy French fries? Steven was going to take her to one of the nicest restaurants in Sweet Valley. Joe couldn't compete with that.

Steven slid back into the booth and ripped open a ketchup packet. "Here you go," he said, handing it to Jill with a smile. But his hand slipped, and ketchup squirted out onto the table, just missing Jill's arm.

"Hey!" she cried. She grabbed a napkin from

the napkin holder and started cleaning up the mess.

"Is that one of those trick ketchups they advertise in the back of comic books?" Megan asked, giggling.

Joe laughed. "Way to go, Wakefield."

"Sorry," Steven said, looking nervously at Jill.

Why can't I do anything right when Jill's around?

Eight

No matter how many times she wrote it down, Jessica still couldn't figure out what had happened to her money. On Tuesday, she had a hundred dollars. It was Thursday night, and she had fifteen dollars. Where did it all go?

Wednesday, she had spent eighteen dollars at Casey's. She had bought a bracelet for Kimberly, hair ribbons for Grace, and a poster for Ellen. That added up to about thirty dollars.

That meant she had spent fifty-five dollars that afternoon! And all she had to show for it was an ugly pair of earrings she didn't even like anymore! She had only bought them because she and Lila had decided they wanted to have identical earrings. After she'd bought things for everyone else, she had to buy something for Lila, too—that had cost her fifteen dollars. Then there were the frozen yogurt cones, the T-shirt Tamara wanted, a tape for Mandy, and special sneaker laces for Belinda.

Writing down the list of what she'd bought practically filled up a whole piece of paper! Jessica put her head in her hands. How was she ever going to explain what had happened to all her money?

The worst thing was that Jessica had to admit that Lila was right. Lila had said that even if Jessica had money, she wouldn't hold onto it. And here she was, with fifteen dollars and twenty-seven cents. It wasn't even enough to buy anything for herself, especially not the shirt at Valley Fashions.

Jessica crumpled up her list of calculations and threw it into the wastebasket. She didn't want anyone else to know all her money was gone—not even Elizabeth.

Jessica tore another sheet of paper out of her social studies notebook and wrote, "How to Get My $100 Back. #1. Return dumb earrings." That would get her at least seven-fifty.

Then she remembered that pierced earrings were not returnable.

"Aunt Helen, can I come in?" Elizabeth knocked gently on the door to the den.

"Sure," Aunt Helen replied.

When Elizabeth walked in and saw her great-aunt sitting in bed with her nightgown on, reading a book, it was hard to imagine that anything was wrong. Aunt Helen looked so relaxed and happy. "How are you?" Elizabeth asked.

"Just fine. I borrowed one of your books." She held up an old Amanda Howard mystery.

"That's a good one," Elizabeth said. She sat down on the edge of the bed. "Aunt Helen, is everything all right?"

"Of course. Why do you ask?"

"I don't know, it's just that you haven't really been acting like yourself," Elizabeth said.

Aunt Helen looked perplexed. "I haven't? Who have I been acting like?"

"I didn't mean it that way," Elizabeth said. "You seem worried about something. Is there anything wrong?"

"I know what this is all about!" Aunt Helen said. "You're worried about your old aunt because you saw me getting all worked up about a TV character. You think I'm turning into a crazy old lady."

"No, I don't!" Elizabeth said. "I just thought maybe there was some kind of problem at home, and that's why you were here."

Aunt Helen gave Elizabeth a strange look. "But you know I planned this trip months ago. Honestly, Elizabeth, I don't know what you're talking about. What sort of problem would there be at home? The only trouble I have is when my neighbor, Mr. Brandon, plants orange flowers that clash with my pink ones." Aunt Helen peered at Elizabeth over the top of her reading glasses. "You know what I think? I think you stayed up too late last night reading your new book. And don't pretend that you weren't, because I went upstairs at about two o'clock, and your light was still on."

Elizabeth grinned. "OK, you caught me. But what were you doing up there in the middle of the night?"

"Oh, I was just a little restless," Aunt Helen said, pulling the covers up higher.

"You mean you couldn't sleep?" Elizabeth asked.

Aunt Helen nodded.

Aha! Elizabeth thought. *So something was bothering her!*

"I don't usually sleep very well in strange beds," Aunt Helen said. "But I have a feeling that tonight, I'll be out in no time." She sat up and patted the pillows behind her head.

"OK," Elizabeth said, standing up. "Sleep well."

Aunt Helen smiled. "Good night, Elizabeth. You'd better get some sleep, or who knows what kind of crazy questions you'll be asking me tomorrow."

"Hey, Jill." Steven stopped at her locker, trying to look like he just happened to be passing by. "How's it going?"

She took out one book and tossed another inside. "OK, except I have to take an algebra test in two minutes."

"They shouldn't be allowed to give tests on Fridays," Steven said.

"I agree!" Jill said, running her hand through her hair. "I was up studying almost all night. It's not exactly my best subject."

Steven took a deep breath and tried to look cool. "I hope you won't be too tired for our date tonight."

"Our date? Oh, right, our date. What are we doing again?" Jill asked.

Well, at least she hadn't completely forgotten about it. "We're going out to dinner," Steven said. "I'm not going to tell you where, but it's going to be nice. Actually, you should wear something, you know, nice. I mean—not that you don't look nice all the time—"

"I know what you mean. Something dressy," Jill said.

"Right," Steven said.

"OK," Jill said.

"I was thinking I'd pick you up around seven," Steven said.

"Pick me up? You don't drive, do you?" Jill's eyes suddenly lit up, and she smiled at him.

Steven had never seen her look so interested in him before. He thought about trying to get a car for the evening. He didn't have a license, so he couldn't rent one, and his parents would never let him use theirs.

"No, not yet," Steven said. "I'm going to get a taxi."

Jill laughed. "You mean your parents. That's what I call my parents, too. Hale Taxi Service."

"No, I'm serious," Steven said.

"Oh, well, OK." The bell rang and Jill shut her locker.

"See you at seven," Steven said as he watched her hurry away down the hall. "Good luck on your test!" he added.

He was psyched—he and Jill had actually had a real conversation, and he hadn't messed up at all. He could tell that Jill was happy that they were going somewhere classy for dinner. Jessica actually knew what she was talking about.

Our date is going to be great, Steven thought. *There's nothing to worry about at all!*

*   *   *

"Jessica, are you going to the mall again today?" Kimberly asked during lunch on Friday.

"Are you kidding," Jessica muttered into her napkin.

"What did you say?"

Jessica put her napkin back in her lap. "Not today. I have to spend some time at home with my aunt."

"Your rich aunt, you mean?" Ellen said.

"She's not rich," Jessica said. "She just believes in giving things to other people." She looked around the table at everyone. She was expecting someone to say, "Just like you, Jessica!" But no one did.

Instead, Kimberly said, "That's too bad. I was looking forward to some more shopping."

"So was I," said Janet.

"Just because I'm not going doesn't mean you can't," Jessica said.

"No, it wouldn't be any fun," Tamara said. She was wearing the T-shirt that Jessica had gotten for her, and it looked fantastic. That only made Jessica feel worse.

"What about tomorrow?" Janet asked. "Let's all meet there—the weather's supposed to be lousy."

"Well, I don't know if I can make it tomorrow, either," Jessica said.

Lila looked at Jessica suspiciously. "I thought the mall was your favorite place in the whole world."

She knows, Jessica thought. "I didn't say I wasn't going to come. I just have to check with my parents first."

"Come on, Jessica, you have to be there," Grace said. "All the Unicorns are going."

"OK, OK!" Jessica said. "I'll be there." She would go, but she wasn't going to bring *any* money. There was no way she was going to spend her last fifteen dollars on anyone but herself.

Nine

◇

"Did your aunt ever work for the government?" Amy asked as she and Elizabeth walked home after school on Friday.

"What do you mean?" Elizabeth asked.

"Last night at dinner my mom was talking about this story she's working on," Amy said. Amy's mother was a reporter for a local television station. "It's all about this guy they're trying to track down who used to be a spy—"

"You think my aunt is a *spy*?" Elizabeth cried.

"It makes sense," Amy said. "See, what my mom was saying was that these spies go to new towns and change their identities—once they stop being spies that is. They have to because if anyone ever found out what they'd been doing, they'd be in trouble. Especially if they're one of those double spies."

"You mean a counterspy?" Elizabeth asked.

"Right. Someone back home must have figured out that your aunt was one of those, and that's why she's here, visiting you. Plus, spies make a lot of money, and she just gave you a whole bunch," Amy concluded.

Elizabeth shook her head. "Aunt Helen's not a spy or a counterspy or anything like that."

"How do you know?" Amy asked. "They're really good at fooling people. She could have fooled you."

Elizabeth pictured her great-aunt in a beige trench coat, creeping around in the fog. Then she burst out laughing. "Amy, that is totally ridiculous! My aunt is not a spy."

Amy looked hurt. "I was just trying to help," she said.

"I know, I'm sorry," Elizabeth said. "It's just—well, you know Aunt Helen."

"If that letter turns out to be from some foreign country, then you won't think my idea was so dumb," Amy said.

When they walked into the Wakefields' house they found Aunt Helen in the living room watching "Days of Turmoil."

"Hi," Elizabeth and Amy said.

"Hello, you two," Aunt Helen said. "I bet you thought you were going to catch me crying again, but you're wrong. Today someone's getting married."

"Aren't you supposed to cry at weddings?" Amy joked.

"Aunt Helen, I wanted to ask your opinion about something," Elizabeth said. "See, we're having this big dance at school in a couple of weeks, and I don't know what to wear."

Aunt Helen seemed surprised. "And you want *my* opinion?"

"She's asking everybody's opinion," Amy said. "She's asked me eight times already."

"I even asked Dad, so you know I'm desperate," Elizabeth added. Actually, there wasn't a dance at school—and if there was, she wouldn't ask for Aunt Helen's or her father's help in deciding what to wear. But she had to get Aunt Helen upstairs somehow!

Aunt Helen got up from the couch.

"I have to call my dad and tell him where I am," Amy said. "I'll be up in a minute, OK?"

"OK," Elizabeth said. She and Aunt Helen went up to her bedroom, and Elizabeth randomly pulled things out of her closet and tossed them on the bed. "There's this skirt, but I don't have a blouse to go with it. Or there's this dress, but I think it makes me look like an eight-year-old. Or I could—"

"Elizabeth!" Amy called up the stairs. "Can you come down? I want some soda, and I can't find the glasses!"

"Go ahead," Aunt Helen said. She picked up some clothes from the bed. "I'll sift through these and see what I can do."

"I'll be right back," Elizabeth said. Then she tore down the steps, taking them three at a time. "What did you find?" she whispered to Amy in the kitchen.

"Nothing," Amy said. "Her suitcase is locked."

"What?" Elizabeth said. She ran into the den with Amy close on her heels. Elizabeth fiddled with the suitcase latch. "You're right, it is. I wonder why she did that."

Amy raised one eyebrow. "Because she's a spy, and spies always do that."

Elizabeth picked up the suitcase. "It feels like it's empty." She shook it a few times, and heard something rattling around inside. "There's not much in there, anyway. Did you look for the key?"

Amy nodded. "I couldn't find it, and I didn't find the letter or anything else."

What could she have done with it? Elizabeth wondered. She felt under the cushions of the sofa bed. Then she looked inside her father's desk. "This is hopeless," she said.

"I'll look," Amy said. "You go back upstairs."

"No. I feel bad enough for snooping around like this," Elizabeth said. "We'd better forget about the letter."

"Wait, we haven't looked in her purse yet," Amy said. She took the purse off the top of the dresser.

"I don't think we should go through that," Elizabeth said. "I'd feel funny."

"Don't you want to find out what's going on?" Amy asked.

"Yes, but—"

"We have to, then." Amy opened the purse and looked through it for a minute, while Elizabeth stood in the doorway and watched to make sure Aunt Helen wasn't coming. "Aha!" Amy said. She pulled out a photograph and showed it to Elizabeth. "Look!"

Elizabeth studied the picture. In it was a man she had never seen before. He was wearing a suit, and he wasn't smiling. "He doesn't look very nice," she said. "I wonder who it is."

"It's probably the same guy who's been bugging her," Amy said. "He looks like a bully, doesn't he? I bet he sent her this picture so she wouldn't forget him. Or it *could* be a picture she took of someone she's spying on!"

"Girls! Are you coming?" Aunt Helen called from the top of the stairs.

Elizabeth shoved the photo back inside Aunt

Helen's purse. "We'll be right there!" she called and turned to Amy. "Maybe it's just a friend of hers."

"Did he look friendly to you?" Amy replied.

"What's that?" Jessica said walking into the Wakefields' kitchen Friday after school as she noticed a box in Steven's hand.

"Nothing," Steven said.

"Come on, you can tell me," Jessica said. "Is it something for your big date tonight?"

Steven turned away from the refrigerator. "How do you know about that?"

"I just know, that's all." Jessica pointed at the box. "So what is it? Candy?"

"No," Steven said, sliding the box into the refrigerator. "It's flowers." He took out a can of soda.

"You did read that article!" Jessica exclaimed. "I knew you would. So where are you taking what's-her-name?"

"Jill, and it's none of your business," Steven replied, heading upstairs.

Jessica trailed after him. "Come on, you can tell me."

"You'll probably show up and try to embarrass me," Steven said. He walked into his room.

"Give me a hint," Jessica said. "It's somewhere fancy, right?"

Steven nodded. "See you."

He was about to shut the door in her face when Jessica said, "So what are you going to wear?" She knew her brother well enough to know that he would have no idea what to wear on a date to a nice restaurant. To him, getting dressed up meant tying his high-top sneakers.

Steven pulled the door back open. "All right, come in," he said.

Jessica smiled and went over to Steven's closet. "I hope you have something decent in here. You might have to borrow something from Dad."

"No way," Steven said. He sat down in his desk chair. "OK, so what am I supposed to wear? A blazer or something, right?"

"What's she wearing?" Jessica asked.

"How am I supposed to know?" Steven said.

"Call her," Jessica said.

Steven shook his head.

"OK, but if you clash, don't blame me." She pulled out a navy blazer and hung it on the doorknob. "Wear this with your tan pants. You'd better iron them, too. Do you have any ties?"

"A couple," Steven said. He got up and searched through his closet for a few minutes. "Maybe I will borrow one from Dad."

"Get a blue-and-red-striped one," Jessica recommended.

"A striped tie? Are you serious?"

"OK, do it yourself then," Jessica snapped. "Go ahead, look like a total fool. See if I care."

"OK, so I'll wear a striped tie," Steven said. "Don't get all bent out of shape."

Jessica glared at her brother for a second, then went back to the closet. "Wear these, too." She tossed Steven's brown loafers out into the room.

"Man, this is going to be harder than I thought," Steven said, nudging the loafers with his feet. "I haven't even worn these before. I'll probably get a blister."

Jessica giggled. "I can't believe I'm giving my brother a *makeover*."

"It's not a makeover," Steven argued. "That's when they put a bunch of makeup on you."

Jessica pretended to study his face. "Well, you could use a little blue eyeliner."

Steven laughed and hit her on the arm. "Cut it out!"

"Did you get her anything besides flowers?" Jessica asked.

"Maybe," Steven said.

"Tell me!" Jessica urged.

"OK, but you have to promise that you won't tell any of your dumb friends about any of this," Steven said. "Especially not Janet. I don't want her to tell Joe—if she does, it'll be all over school. If you tell anyone, you'll be sorry."

"My lips are sealed," Jessica said. "So what did you get her? Is it jewelry?"

"Earrings," Steven said. "They're real gold, too." He took the box out of his desk and showed it to Jessica. "Pretty impressive, huh?"

"Did you spend your whole hundred dollars on this date or what?" Jessica asked.

"Practically," Steven said. "Actually, I think I'll have some left over."

"Really?" Jessica said. "In that case, how about some money for your fashion consultant."

"You mean you?" Steven asked.

Jessica nodded. "If it hadn't been for me, you'd end up looking like a nerd on your big date. The whole thing would have been totally ruined once Jill saw you standing there in your old plaid blazer—"

"All right already." Steven took his wallet out of his jeans pocket and handed Jessica a ten-dollar bill.

Jessica thought she must be seeing things. Steven had never given her any money before, and she had asked many times. "Boy, you *must* be in love!" she said, running to the door before Steven could change his mind.

Steven heard a car honk its horn outside the house. He took one last look at himself in the mirror, checked to make sure he had Jill's gift in

the pocket of his blazer, and then rushed downstairs. The rest of the family was in the kitchen,
making dinner.

"My, don't you look handsome!" Aunt Helen
exclaimed.

"Who is this person?" Mr. Wakefield said,
grabbing Steven's arm. "Excuse me, do you live
here?"

"Cut it out, Dad," Steven said.

"Yeah, you might wrinkle his jacket," Jessica
teased.

Steven opened the refrigerator and grabbed
the corsage.

"Where did you decide to take her?" Mrs.
Wakefield asked.

"Jacqueline's," Steven said, just as the horn
honked again.

"Really?" Mrs. Wakefield seemed surprised.
"It's awfully expensive, you know."

"I know, Mom," Steven said as he hurried to
the door.

"That's the point," Elizabeth said.

"I'm glad someone's having fun with their
money!" Aunt Helen said.

"Don't worry, I will!" Steven called over his
shoulder. He opened the door of the taxicab and
slid into the back seat. "Hi. One-sixteen Madison
Street," he told the driver.

Steven double-checked to make sure he had his

wallet, then settled back into the seat. He felt a little nervous, but he told himself that it would pass.

The cab pulled up in front of Jill's house five minutes later. "Wait here—we'll be right out," Steven said. He felt like he was in a movie as he got out of the car. People were always taking cabs in movies.

He rang the doorbell and held the corsage box behind his back so he could surprise Jill. No one answered, so he rang it again. Then he waited another minute.

"Looks like you got stood up!" the cab driver yelled out the window.

Steven turned around and glared at him. Suddenly, the door opened, catching Steven off guard.

"Hi," Jill said. "Sorry it took me so long. I thought my dad was down here but I guess he went out."

Steven laughed nervously. "No problem."

"Come inside for a second, I have to get my jacket," Jill said.

When Steven stepped into the house and got a good look at Jill, he was glad Jessica had helped him pick out what to wear. Jill looked absolutely perfect. She was wearing a sleeveless green dress, which made her look older than she was, and a pretty gold necklace.

"Uh, this is for you." Steven held out the box, and Jill took it and looked inside.

"How pretty," Jill said. "Thanks." She took the white rose out of the box. "Can you help me pin it?"

"Pin it?" Steven repeated.

"To my dress," Jill said.

"Right," Steven said. He took a few steps toward her, and she handed him the flower. Steven's hands were shaking as he grabbed the pin from the box and tried to slip it through the fabric of Jill's dress.

"Ouch!" Jill cried, jumping back.

Steven felt his face turn red. "Sorry." *How could I be so clumsy*, he thought.

"Maybe this wasn't such a hot idea. Here, I'll carry it," Jill said. Steven gave her the corsage, and she grabbed her pocketbook from a chair near the door.

"Here's your jacket." Steven held it up so she could slip into it. At least he managed to do that without messing it up.

And now, on with the dream date! Steven said to himself as he followed Jill down the Hales' sidewalk to the cab.

Ten

◇

"I didn't know you were staying over at Amy's tonight," Jessica said.

Elizabeth stuffed her nightshirt into a small duffel bag. "I guess I forgot to tell you."

"What am I going to do all night?" Jessica complained.

"Why don't you call Lila?" Elizabeth suggested.

"No way!" Jessica said.

Elizabeth turned to her. "Did you guys have a fight or something?"

"N-no," Jessica said. "By the way, did you go shopping today?"

Elizabeth put a pair of socks into the bag. "Nope. Why?"

"I was just wondering if you still had a lot of money left," Jessica said.

Elizabeth nodded.

"Are you still going to buy a camera?" Jessica asked.

"I don't know," Elizabeth said. She grabbed her brush from her dresser. "Jess, have you noticed anything strange about Aunt Helen?" she suddenly asked.

"What do you mean?"

Elizabeth shrugged. "I just thought, you know, maybe something was wrong with her."

"Yeah, she broke her arm," Jessica said, "remember?"

"Not that. I don't know. She's just seemed really quiet, like she doesn't want to talk about anything, and she's hardly been out of the house since she's been here."

"Well, she's not exactly young," Jessica said.

"I know, but that's never stopped her before."

Jessica didn't know what Elizabeth was talking about. "Why are you so worried?"

"I'm not worried," Elizabeth said.

"Could have fooled me," Jessica said.

Elizabeth chewed her thumbnail for a minute. "You know that letter she got? Where do you think that was from?"

Jessica shrugged. "I don't know. Maybe it was a friend who really misses her. It could have been the bank, too."

"The bank?" Elizabeth asked.

"Sure," Jessica said. "Maybe she forgot to bring enough money with her so she asked them to send some."

"I don't think so," Elizabeth said. "They wouldn't send money through the mail like that."

"OK, what do *you* think it was?" Jessica asked.

"I don't know."

"Then why are you so worried?" Jessica couldn't see why Elizabeth was making such a big deal about such a small package. "It might not even be a letter," she said. "Maybe Aunt Helen forgot to bring something and so she had to have someone send it to her. You know, like her false teeth or something."

"Jessica!" Elizabeth laughed and threw a pillow at her sister.

"Well, it could be," Jessica said, giggling. "That's probably why she didn't want to tell us what was in it."

"I have to get going," Elizabeth said, slinging her bag over her shoulder. "Amy rented a movie and we want to watch it before 'Staying Up With Bob' comes on."

"I'm going to watch it tonight, too," Jessica said. "Everyone at school keeps talking about it, and I haven't even seen it yet."

"I hope it's as funny as everyone says. I could use a good laugh," Elizabeth said.

"If it isn't, just picture Steven on his big date. Now *that's* funny!" Jessica said.

"Hi, we have a reservation," Steven told the man in the tuxedo who met them at the door of Jacqueline's. Steven had chosen a French restaurant after Jill told him she used to live in France.

"You do?" the man said, giving Steven and Jill the once-over. "Are you meeting your parents here?"

"No," Steven said, irritated. "The last name is Wakefield."

The man checked the large black book on the table in front of him. "I see," he said. "In that case, let me show you to your table." He led them through the crowded restaurant to a small table in the back. He pulled out Jill's chair for her. "Enjoy," he said as he walked away.

Steven shot him a dirty look. "That waiter was a jerk," he said. "He didn't even give us menus."

"He's the maitre d'," Jill said.

"The what?"

"That's what they call the host—it's French,"

Jill said. She looked around the room at the other tables.

"I know some Spanish, but that's about it," Steven said. "I plan to take French next year, though." He thought that would impress her.

"Don't bother," she said, "it's boring."

So much for that topic. Steven looked up as a waiter arrived with two menus. "Here you are, sir," he said. "Would you like to see a wine list?" The waiter slapped Steven on the back. "Just kidding."

Does everyone in this restaurant have to humiliate me? Steven thought as he took the menu and opened it to the first page. His eyes almost crossed as he looked at the prices. Five dollars for a bowl of onion soup? And that was the cheapest thing on the menu—except for soft drinks, which were two seventy-five. Most of the dinners were from fifteen to thirty dollars. Steven only had forty-five dollars, after the cab ride ended up costing him almost twenty.

I'm going to starve, Steven thought.

"So what are you going to have?" he asked Jill, trying to sound calm. *Please don't order an appetizer.*

"I don't know." Jill ran her finger down the menu. "The beef bourguignon sounds good, but so does the duck l'orange."

Steven casually glanced at his menu. If Jill

ordered either one of those, he'd be having onion soup. He hated onions.

The waiter returned to take their order. "Miss?" he prompted Jill, who was still studying her menu.

"I'd like the cassoulet," she said. "Please."

Steven felt his shoulders relax. Jill had chosen one of the least expensive meals on the menu.

"How about an appetizer?" the waiter asked. Steven felt like kicking him under the table.

"No thank you," Jill said. "But I'll have a sparkling mineral water."

"Very well," the waiter said, writing that down. "And for you?" he asked Steven.

"Oh, um, I'll have what she's having," Steven said. He didn't know exactly what that was, but at least he could afford it. "And a glass of water—regular water."

The waiter looked down his nose at Steven, then took their menus and went off to the kitchen.

"So," Steven said, looking around the restaurant. It wasn't quite as exciting as he'd hoped it would be, but it was pretty fancy. "I told you we weren't going to the Valley Diner." He smiled at Jill.

"This place is pretty nice," Jill said. "A little old-fashioned, but nice."

Two points for the phone book, Steven thought.

He had looked up "Restaurants—French" the night before, and Jacqueline's had a big listing.

"Yeah, there are a lot of old-timers here," Steven said, gesturing to a table next to them.

"You look like a different person when you wear a jacket and tie," Jill observed.

"Really? Is that good or bad?" Steven asked, feeling happy that she had noticed.

"Just different, that's all. Older, I guess."

Steven leaned back in his chair. "Well, I am almost fifteen." He tried to make his voice sound deeper, like it sometimes did.

"Pretty soon you can get your learner's permit," Jill said.

"I know. I can't wait," Steven said.

Then they sat there for a few minutes in total silence. Steven couldn't think of a thing to say. The waiter brought their water, and Steven sipped his slowly, stalling until he could think of something.

"Look, there's a little dance floor up there," Jill suddenly said. She pointed over Steven's shoulder.

He turned around and looked behind him. There were five or six couples twirling around to a jazzy tune.

"I love dancing," Jill said. "Of course, my favorite kind is square dancing."

"Really," Steven said, smiling. *Square dancing?*

He liked Jill a lot, but he didn't know if he could deal with square dancing. Back in middle school, they'd had to learn it in gym class. He liked it about as much as he liked onion soup.

"Come on, let's go dance," Jill said. She stood up.

"But our food will be here soon," Steven said. "We should probably wait here."

"No, it won't. It always takes forever at fancy restaurants." Jill held out her hand. "Come on, it'll be fun."

Steven stood up and took Jill's hand. "We don't have to do-si-do or anything, do we?"

Jill giggled. "You're so funny. Come on." She and Steven walked over to the dance floor.

"I don't think there's enough room," Steven said.

"Sure there is," Jill said. She gently pushed him out onto the dance floor.

Steven frantically tried to remember the other dance steps he'd learned in middle school. Was it two steps up, one—"Whoops," he said smashing into Jill.

"You're supposed to go that way," she said, pointing.

"I'm a little rusty," Steven said. "It's been a while since I last went dancing."

"Just relax and do this," Jill said. She glided

gracefully to one side and then the other, while Steven stood there like a rock. "It's easy."

Steven watched her carefully, then joined in. He took two steps forward, two steps to the side and—

"Ouch!" Jill cried, for the second time that night. She limped off the dance floor. Several people who were dancing stopped and stared at Steven.

The food better be good, he thought as he followed Jill back to their table.

Elizabeth propped her feet on the coffee table and leaned back on the couch. She was ready to relax and stop thinking about Aunt Helen for a while. Talking to Jessica had made her feel better. If Jessica didn't think there was anything to worry about, then maybe there wasn't.

"What movie did you get?" Elizabeth asked.

Amy put a bowl of popcorn down on the table. "By the time my mom could take me to the video store there was hardly anything left. The guy at the store recommended this." She put the tape into the VCR and pressed the play button. "He said it was a classic."

"What's it called?" Elizabeth asked.

Amy picked up the cassette case. *"Don't Talk."*

"What's it about?"

"It's based on a true story, some famous court case or something," Amy said as the opening titles came on the screen. She dropped onto the couch next to Elizabeth and grabbed a handful of popcorn.

The first part of the movie kept switching back and forth between two different people's lives. Neither of them was very exciting in Elizabeth's opinion. She was just about to ask Amy if she wanted to watch TV, when there was a loud bang—somebody had been killed!

"Yuck," Amy said. "I hate blood."

"It's not real," Elizabeth reminded her. She and Amy went through the same routine every time they watched a movie together.

"See the guy standing across the street in the donut shop?" Amy said. "He just saw the whole thing. He knows who did it. Can you imagine, seeing someone get killed?"

"And the killer saw the witness!" Elizabeth exclaimed. She looked thoughtfully at Amy for a moment. "That's the same thing that happened in Aunt Helen's soap opera," Elizabeth said. "Remember?—Oh, no!" Elizabeth cried, jumping to her feet. "Aunt Helen! Don't you get it? This could be exactly what's going on with her!"

"You mean she witnessed a crime?" Amy asked. "And someone knows about it."

"Yes!" Elizabeth said. "It all makes sense. She's trying to hide at our house, only they found her and sent her that threatening letter. They probably followed her to the airport. She's hardly been outside the whole time she's been visiting! She's probably too afraid."

"I bet they broke her arm, too!" Amy added. "I bet it was that mean man in the picture who did it. To keep her from saying anything to the police!"

"And that's why she was crying so hard about what was happening on 'Days of Turmoil,' " Elizabeth said. "Because the same thing was happening to her. She thought she was going to get killed like that nurse did!"

"Your poor aunt!" Amy cried.

"Come on," Elizabeth said, grabbing her jacket. "We have to get back to my house and make sure Aunt Helen is safe!"

Eleven

◈

"I'll have a piece of the chocolate mousse torte."

Steven felt all of his stomach muscles tighten into a knot. He had just added up everything they'd had, and he knew he had enough to cover it. But now what? The dessert prices weren't even listed on the menu—and he couldn't tell Jill *not* to get dessert. That would ruin the whole evening. After the disaster on the dance floor, he and Jill had actually been having a conversation. Steven hadn't done anything dumb in nearly an hour, but this could really finish him off.

"Here you are," the waiter said, placing a sliver of pie in front of Jill. "And here you are." He put a small tray down next to Steven's glass of water. On it was the bill.

"They sure didn't give you a very big piece,"

Steven remarked. He was glad—that meant it wouldn't cost very much.

"It's so rich you can only eat a little," Jill said. She took a dainty bite. "Mmm . . . delicious."

"I could probably eat a lot more than that," Steven said.

"Why don't you get a piece?" Jill asked. "Tell them to make it big."

"No, that's OK." Steven shook his head. "I'm full."

"Steven, do you have an after-school job?" Jill asked.

"No," Steven said, "do you?"

"No. I was just wondering how you could afford to take me out to a place like this," Jill said.

"Oh. Well, I save a lot," Steven said. He thought that sounded better than the truth. The only money he usually saved was pennies—he had tons of them under his bed. Steven reached over and picked up the check. "Anyway, this isn't that expen—whoa!"

"Whoa what?" Jill asked.

Steven looked at her, still reeling from the shock of seeing the bill. "Ah, whoa, I didn't realize how late it was." He tapped his watch. "It's almost ten o'clock."

Jill nodded. "We've been here a long time."

Yeah, and they must be charging by the hour! Steven thought, examining the bill. There was Jill's dinner, and his dinner, and Jill's mineral water—and that microscopic piece of pie cost seven dollars! Steven checked the addition on the bill. Unfortunately, it was right. Everything added up to fifty dollars. Steven had forty-five.

If only I hadn't given Jessica that ten dollars! How did I let her talk me into that, anyway?

"That was so good." Jill dabbed the corners of her mouth with a napkin. "Thank you."

Steven nodded. He looked desperately around the restaurant, hoping to spot one of his father's friends who could loan him the extra money. He could see it now. Jill's father would have to come pick her up because Steven would be stuck inside the kitchen, working to pay off the rest of the bill!

There was only one thing to do—stall. "I almost forgot," Steven said. "I mean, I wanted to wait until after dinner to give these to you." He took the earrings out of his blazer pocket and handed them to Jill.

"What a pretty box!" she said.

For a split second Steven thought about asking for them back. Maybe the restaurant would accept them as payment!

Jill unwrapped the package and lifted the lid off the box. "Oh," she said, taking out the earrings. "These are nice."

"Do you like them?" Steven asked. Then he checked to make sure Jill had pierced ears. She did, all right. The earrings she was wearing were the same as the ones he had just given her!

"Yeah, I like them a lot," Jill said. "I have some that are kind of like them, but they're not exactly the same."

"I noticed," Steven mumbled. "Sorry."

"That's OK," Jill said. "I can use them. Thanks."

Steven drummed his fingers on the table. He didn't know how he was going to say what he had to say. It was too humiliating, especially on top of all the other blunders he'd made that evening. Jill would probably never go out with him again.

"So, should we go?" Jill put the earrings back in the box. "I told my father I'd be home by ten-thirty. We could ask the maitre d' to call a cab for us."

Steven bit his lower lip. "We could," he said. "Uh, but there's one small problem."

"You lost their number? That's OK, he can look it up," Jill said.

"No," Steven said. "It's well, well, I hate to ask you this, but do you have any money with you?"

Elizabeth threw open the door and ran through the kitchen into the living room. "Aunt Helen!" she cried, rushing over to her. "Don't worry, everything will be OK."

Aunt Helen looked at Elizabeth in alarm. "What are you talking about?"

Amy ran into the room, panting. "We'll protect you," she said, barely able to get the words out.

"Protect her from what?" Mr. and Mrs. Wakefield both said at the same time.

"Is this a practical joke?" Jessica asked. She was lying on the floor in front of the TV.

"No, it's not a joke at all," Elizabeth said. "Aunt Helen, why didn't you tell us?"

"Tell you what?" Aunt Helen replied. She looked genuinely confused.

"It's OK, you can talk here," Amy said. "Nobody will hear. I checked around the outside of the house, and it's all clear."

Aunt Helen shook her head. "Is it me, or are these two girls not making any sense?"

"Elizabeth, why don't you stop fooling around and explain what you're talking about," Mr. Wakefield said. "We want to get back to our movie."

"We were watching a movie over at Amy's house, and all of a sudden I realized that it was just like your life, Aunt Helen," Elizabeth said.

"Sounds like a thrilling movie," Jessica joked. "No wonder you came over here."

"Jessica, this is serious!" Elizabeth said. "Aunt Helen is here hiding from a killer!"

Mrs. Wakefield laughed. "Come on, Elizabeth. You've been reading too much of your new Amanda Howard book."

"No, I haven't," Elizabeth insisted. "It's true! Amy and I figured the whole thing out."

Amy nodded. "See, Aunt Helen witnessed a big crime, and the person who committed the crime knows that she saw it. Just like on 'Days of Turmoil'!"

"So they've been threatening to keep her quiet," Elizabeth continued. "That's how your arm got broken," she told Aunt Helen.

"What makes you think that?" Jessica asked.

"Because, she never told us how she did it. Every time we asked about it, she changed the subject," Elizabeth said. "Then one night I overheard her talking to Dad about how someone was trying to bully her and how she might have to get a lawyer to protect her. Then she got that threat in the mail!"

Aunt Helen was shaking her head. "Oh, Elizabeth, I am so sorry," she said. She reached out and gave Elizabeth a hug.

"I wish you would have just told us the truth from the beginning," Elizabeth said.

Aunt Helen stroked Elizabeth's hair. "You're right. I should have told you the truth," she said. "But that story you just told is not the truth."

"It's not?"

"Is the truth *worse*?" Amy asked.

Aunt Helen took a deep breath. "I suppose I should have told you as soon as I got here, but I didn't want to worry you. Your parents agreed to keep my secret, although they thought you might be suspicious. Now, don't worry—no criminal is after me, and I'm not in any danger. But I got into a car accident last week. It wasn't too serious. However, that is how I broke my arm."

"What about the letter you got?" Elizabeth asked.

"That was from my insurance company," Aunt Helen said. "I have an insurance policy on my car so that I get reimbursed for any damage. Well, unfortunately, the insurance company claims that they didn't receive my last check, and they say they're not going to give me any money to repair my car. There's almost two thousand dollars worth of damage!"

"What that means is, Aunt Helen has to prove that she did make all of her payments to them," Mrs. Wakefield explained. "If she can't, she'll be stuck with a very large repair bill!"

"That doesn't make any sense," Elizabeth said. "If you were worried about money, why did you just give us so much?"

Aunt Helen shrugged her shoulders. "My

accident wasn't too serious, but it did scare me. I was just so happy to be all right afterward that I wanted to share my happiness."

"Well, if you need any money, I still have seventy dollars," Elizabeth offered.

"No!" Aunt Helen said. "I don't need that money."

"Phew," Jessica said. "Because I—well, let's just say I don't have that much."

"That's some theory you came up with!" Mr. Wakefield said.

"I guess it sounds silly to you now, but it made a lot of sense to us," Elizabeth said. "You were acting so differently, Aunt Helen, I knew something was up."

"I've been taking it easy since the accident," Aunt Helen explained. "It took a lot out of me."

"I have a question," Elizabeth said. "But before I ask it, I want to make sure I won't get into trouble."

"This sounds good," Jessica said, sitting up.

"OK." Aunt Helen nodded. "What?"

"Well, we found this picture in your pocketbook," Elizabeth said, "and we thought it was a picture of the man who was threatening you. He didn't look very nice," she added quickly. "He was kind of scowling, actually. Who is that?"

Aunt Helen giggled and her face turned bright pink. "That's Thomas," she said.

"The same Thomas you always go to the movies with?" Mrs. Wakefield asked.

Aunt Helen nodded.

"That's your boyfriend?" Amy asked. "I mean, your man friend, or, whatever."

"He doesn't like to smile for pictures," Aunt Helen said. "He says he looks silly when he smiles. I'll have to tell him that you thought he was a criminal!"

"Do you feel better now, Elizabeth?" Mr. Wakefield asked, smiling. "Or do you want to check and see if the phones are bugged?"

"Well, at least we know one thing now for sure," Aunt Helen said. "Elizabeth is going to be a great mystery writer some day. I mean, no one but a mystery writer could have come up with that plot!"

Elizabeth laughed. "Maybe I'd better stick to writing and forget about being a detective."

Just then the door opened, and then slammed shut. Steven walked into the living room, took off his blazer, and threw it on the floor.

"How was your date, or should I ask?" Mrs. Wakefield said.

"Terrible," Steven replied. He turned and glared at Jessica. "And it's all your fault!"

"Me? What did I do?" Jessica answered.

"First you tell me to go to this ritzy restaurant, then you talk me out of ten bucks right before I go," he said. "Thanks a lot!"

"You *gave* me the money," Jessica argued. "I didn't make you do it."

Steven let out a deep sigh and sank into the big chair by the TV.

"That bad, huh?" Mr. Wakefield said.

"Put it this way, Dad. I had to take the bus home," Steven grumbled.

"What about Jill? How did she get home?" Elizabeth asked.

"Her father came and picked her up at the restaurant. *After* he told me what an irresponsible jerk I was," Steven said.

Elizabeth tried as hard as she could not to smile.

"Did you two have a nice time before that?" Mrs. Wakefield asked.

Steven rolled his eyes. "It was a nightmare from the beginning. First I went to her house, only she wasn't ready, so the cab ended up costing me twenty dollars. Then I tried to put her dumb corsage on, and I jabbed her with the pin."

Elizabeth snickered, and Steven frowned at her. "Sorry," she said. She cleared her throat loudly.

"Then it turned out they had dancing at this restaurant, and she loves to dance," Steven went on. "You know, like ballroom dancing."

"But you don't know how," Mrs. Wakefield said.

"Right. I think I only broke two of her toes." Steven loosened his tie. "Meanwhile, everyone at the restaurant is treating me like I'm six years old. Then I gave her these earrings I bought for her, but it turned out she already has the exact same pair—she was *wearing* them."

Jessica slapped her hand over her mouth to keep from laughing. Elizabeth could hear Aunt Helen giggling, too.

"*Then*, the bill came," Steven said. "I had to borrow fifteen dollars from Jill."

Jessica jumped up from the floor. "Don't say anything else until I get back." She ran upstairs, and a minute later she returned. She walked over to Steven and held out her hand. "Here's your ten dollars so you can pay her back tomorrow."

Steven looked up at her and smiled. "Some dream date, huh?"

"Definitely a nightmare," Jessica said.

"Whatever you do, don't tell Janet Howell what happened," Steven said. "Not you, or you, or you." He pointed to Elizabeth and Amy, too.

"We won't," Jessica said. "I mean, do you think we want everyone to know what a dweeb we have for a brother?"

Steven grabbed her arm and twisted it behind her back. "What did you say?"

"I said, we're so lucky to have such a great brother!" Jessica squealed.

"OK then." He let go of her. "Hey, it's almost time for 'Staying Up With Bob.' " He reached over and changed the TV channel.

"So much for our movie," Mr. Wakefield said to Aunt Helen.

"That's OK, you're all entertaining enough," Aunt Helen replied. "Who needs a movie? We've got a mystery, a romance—"

"A *dead* romance," Steven corrected her. He stood up and walked toward the kitchen.

"Where are you going?" Mrs. Wakefield asked. "I thought you wanted to watch this show."

"I do, but I need some food first," Steven said, kicking off his loafers. "All I had to eat tonight was a miserable piece of casserole and a glass of water! I blew all my money on dinner, and I'm starving."

"Next time, take her to the Dairi Burger," Jessica suggested.

Twelve

◇

"Hi, Jessica!" Tamara said. "We thought maybe you weren't coming."

"Yeah, we agreed to meet here at eleven o'clock," Janet said. She and the rest of the Unicorns were standing by the fountain in the middle of the mall.

"I know, but I was up really late last night," Jessica explained. "Sorry—I overslept a little."

"I was just looking at this necklace I want to get," Kimberly said. "It would go really well with my new bracelet. Want to see it?"

Jessica shrugged. "Sure." Since she wasn't going to buy anything, either for herself or anyone else, it didn't really matter where they went. She wanted to pick up a thank-you card to give to Aunt Helen, but that was it.

"Great!" Kimberly started walking toward

one of the trendy jewelry stores nearby, and Jessica followed her, along with the rest of the group.

Inside the store, Kimberly held up a long necklace made of sparkling beads. "See? Isn't it great?"

Jessica nodded. "It's pretty."

"I think it would look really good if I wore the two of them together." Kimberly slipped the necklace over her head and admired her reflection in the mirror. "What do you think, Jessica?"

"It looks nice." Jessica started looking at some of the earrings. They were pretty cheap, and she thought it might be a good way to spend the rest of her money.

"Earrings—hey, that's a great idea!" Kimberly said. "I could get earrings to match, too." She took a pair of long, dangling earrings off one of the displays and held them up against her ears. "How do they look?"

"Nice," Ellen said. "I wish I had some like that."

"I think I'll get the necklace and the earrings," Kimberly said.

"Just don't wear them all at once," Janet advised.

"You're right," Kimberly said. She took her wallet out of her raincoat pocket. "Oh no!" she said, looking toward Jessica. "I only have two dollars." She checked the price tag on the necklace. "This is five, and the earrings are four."

Jessica just kept looking at the earrings. She held some red and white polka-dotted ones up against her hair.

"I guess I'll just get the necklace, then," Kimberly said. She stood beside Jessica.

Jessica could tell that Kimberly was waiting for her to pull some money out of her sock, but she wasn't going to give in. Even though she really liked buying things for her friends, those days were over.

When Jessica didn't respond, Kimberly said, "What's the matter, don't you think I should get it?"

"No, I really like it," Jessica said, smiling at her. "You should get it if you want it."

Kimberly studied her expression. She put the necklace back in the display case.

"Let's go to that T-shirt place," Ellen said. "I want to see if they have any unicorn appliqués that they can put on shirts."

"That's a great idea," Tamara said. "We could all get purple T-shirts with our names on the back, or else just with a little unicorn in the corner.

Jessica almost burst out laughing. Did they really think that she was going to outfit everyone with a T-shirt? What was she, a bank? They just expected her to give and give.

"I think that's going to be pretty expensive," Lila said. For once, Jessica agreed with Lila completely.

"Well, we can *look*," Ellen said. "Then we'll decide. Right, Jessica?"

"Whatever," Jessica said.

Ellen and the rest of the group walked into the T-shirt store.

Jessica was about to follow them when Lila grabbed her arm. "Hold on a second, I want to talk to you," she said.

Jessica turned to her friend.

"You ran out of money, didn't you?" Lila whispered. "That's why you didn't buy that necklace for Kimberly. It's OK, I won't tell anybody. But they're going to find out pretty soon."

"No, I didn't run out of money," Jessica said. Not completely, anyway—she still had her fifteen dollars.

"But you don't have a whole lot left," Lila said. "I know. I saw all that stuff you bought for everybody. It adds up. And the worst thing is, they don't even care."

"You're right, it does add up." Jessica shrugged. "Well, easy come, easy go."

"Huh?" Lila stared at Jessica.

"I got really upset when I realized I'd spent so much money on everybody," Jessica explained. "But then I figured, I was just kind of passing it on. Aunt Helen gave it to me, so I'd give it to everyone else." Jessica smiled at the puzzled expression on Lila's face. She liked watching Lila go crazy.

"Are you serious?" Lila asked. "You don't care that you're broke again?"

"It's only money," Jessica said.

"Jessica, Lila! You have to come in here and see these purple T-shirts!" Ellen called to them from inside the store.

"We can look, right?" Jessica walked into the store and over to the group. Behind her, she could hear Lila muttering, "It's only money?"

About an hour later, Jessica wandered into the card store. No one was too interested in shopping after they'd figured out that her shopping spree was over. But they had made a plan to meet up later at Casey's.

Inside the card store, Jessica spotted a familiar face looking at the picture frames. "Hi, Jess," Elizabeth said when she spotted her. "What are you doing here?"

"I was going to get a card for Aunt Helen. What about you?" Jessica asked.

"Me, too. Then I thought I'd get her a little picture frame so she could put a picture of Thomas in it instead of just sticking that photo in her purse." Elizabeth held up a small silver frame. "Do you think this is nice?"

Jessica nodded. "How much is it?"

"It's fifteen," Elizabeth said.

"I'll pitch in half," Jessica said.

"Are you sure? I thought you didn't have much money left."

"How did you know that?"

"I figured if you got ten dollars out of Steven, you probably did ask for it," Elizabeth said. "And you probably wanted it for something."

"I didn't need it," Jessica said. "It's just that there's this shirt I want to get. But it's forty dollars and I only have fifteen."

"You spent eighty-five dollars? On what?" Elizabeth asked.

"I don't know," Jessica said. "I bought a T-shirt for Tamara, a bracelet for Kimberly, a poster for Ellen—"

"I get the picture," Elizabeth said. "You don't have to pitch in on this if you don't want to."

"No, I want to," Jessica said. "Hey, did you get your camera?" She pointed to the bag from Carsten's Camera in Elizabeth's hand.

Elizabeth nodded. "I got the exact kind I wanted. It's so cool, and it was even on sale."

"Let me see it," Jessica said.

Elizabeth took a box out of the bag, and then pulled the camera out of its box. "It's thirty-five millimeter, and it has auto focus and auto rewind," she explained, pointing to various buttons. "It's really easy to use, and it's so small, I can carry it around with me all the time if I want."

"How much was it?" Jessica asked.

"Eighty-five dollars," Elizabeth said. "They gave me a free case for it, too."

"So you spent eighty-five, too," Jessica said.

"Yeah, but I'd already saved fifty," Elizabeth replied as they walked up to the cash register. "So out of Aunt Helen's money I really only spent sixty-five. Thirty-five for the camera and thirty for the new Amanda Howard book and some other stuff.

Jessica quickly picked out a thank-you card for Aunt Helen. Then she and Elizabeth paid for the picture frame and their cards and waited while the clerk wrapped the frame in a gift box.

"Thanks," Elizabeth said, taking the bag from the clerk. "What are you going to do now, Jess? Do you want to go to Valley Fashions? That shirt might be on sale."

Jessica held up the rest of her money. "For seven dollars? I doubt it."

"Maybe not, but if it looks good on you, it'll look good on me, right?" Elizabeth said.

Jessica frowned. She didn't like the idea of Elizabeth wearing the shirt she wanted to get. "I guess," she muttered.

"We could be co-owners of the shirt," Elizabeth suggested. "I'll give you the rest of the money for it, but we'll both own it. So I get to wear it, too."

Jessica wrinkled her nose. "Everyone at school would get really sick of it!"

"I guess you're right," Elizabeth said as they walked through the mall. "How about if I give you the rest of the money for it, and you give me that blue sweatshirt you bought when we visited Dad's college. You've hardly ever worn it, and it's practically brand-new."

Jessica's eyes lit up. She was going to have a brand-new, totally cool blouse, for only seven dollars. "That's a great idea, Elizabeth. You know, I don't think this shirt is your style, anyway." They walked into Valley Fashions, and Jessica took it off the rack.

Elizabeth shook her head. "Definitely not. I'll take the sweatshirt. Look, it's on sale, too—ten dollars off."

"Great!" Jessica said. "Then you only need to give me twenty-three dollars. Plus a little for tax. Thanks!"

After they bought the blouse, Jessica and Elizabeth walked back out into the mall. "See, now we both have something to show for our hundred bucks," Elizabeth said.

A few minutes later, the girls headed to Casey's. Since it was pouring rain outside, the place was packed.

"I think I see Todd over there," Elizabeth said. "I'm going to talk to him, OK?"

"Sure," Jessica said. "And thanks for helping me buy my shirt."

"No problem," Elizabeth said. She walked over to Todd's table.

Jessica scanned the tables until she saw Lila sitting in the corner by herself.

"I thought you might show up early," Lila said. "I know you can't last long without food."

"Very funny," Jessica said, sitting down at the table. The waiter came over, and she ordered a hot fudge sundae.

"What did you get?" Lila asked, pointing to Jessica's bag. "Socks or something?"

"No, it's that blouse I wanted," Jessica said. "I made a deal with Elizabeth. Here comes everyone else."

"Hi, Jessica," Mandy said, swinging into a chair beside her. When everyone was assembled Mandy pushed a small box across the table to Jessica.

"What is it?" Jessica asked.

"Open it," Kimberly urged.

Jessica lifted the top off the box. Inside were the polka-dotted earrings she had been looking at earlier! "Are these for me?" she asked.

"Of course they're for you!" Tamara said.

"Thanks," Jessica said. "That was really nice."

"Not half as nice as all the things you did for us," Mandy said. "We just wanted to show you how much we appreciated your taking us on *your* shopping spree."

"We would have gotten you something more expensive, but everyone could only pitch in a dollar," Grace explained.

"That's OK, I love these," Jessica said, running her fingers over the earrings. "Thanks!"

When the girls had finished their sundaes, Jessica picked up her bill and reached in her pocket for money. *Uh-oh*, she thought. She was down to twenty-seven cents. She stood up and looked around Casey's for Elizabeth and Todd, but she didn't see them anywhere.

Lila sighed loudly. "How much do you need?" she asked, taking out her change purse.

"Two dollars?" Jessica said, looking timidly at Lila.

"Some things never change," Lila said. She took the bills out of her purse and gave them to Jessica.

"I'll pay you back tomorrow," Jessica promised.

Lila got up and picked up her bags. "It's OK, you don't have to," she said. "My treat."

Jessica stared at her. "Some things *do* change!"

Steven took a deep breath and held his hands out in front of him to try to stop them from shaking. Then he rang the doorbell. The second he pushed the button, he wished he hadn't. He wanted to just leave the envelope on the doorstep and ride away on his bike.

"Hello," Mrs. Hale said, opening the door wide.

"Uh, hello," Steven replied. "I'm Steven Wakefield. I came by to drop something off for Jill."

Mrs. Hale took a step back. "So you're Steven Wakefield," she said, looking critically at him.

Steven smiled nervously. Mrs. Hale had probably heard all about his date with Jill the night before.

"Come in from the rain," Mrs. Hale said.

"I just wanted to—"

"Don't be silly. You're getting soaked out there," Mrs. Hale said.

"Is, uh, Jill home?" he asked, stepping into the front hallway.

"She sure is," Mrs. Hale said. "I'll get her for you."

"That's OK," Steven said. "I can leave this—"

"Jill!" Mrs. Hale yelled up the stairs. "Jill! You have a visitor!"

Steven caught a glimpse of his reflection in the mirror over the couch. He'd gotten caught in a downpour on the way over, and his hair was stuck to his forehead in wet clumps. He ran his fingers through his hair and tried to straighten it out.

A few minutes later, Jill came down the stairs. When she saw Steven, her face clouded over. "Oh, it's you," she said.

"Hi, Jill." Steven said. "Sorry about last night."

Jill toyed with the necklace she was wearing. "I've had better dates."

Steven reached into his jacket pocket and took out the envelope. "Here's the money I borrowed last night," he said.

She took the soggy envelope and looked at it suspiciously.

"I got caught in the rain," Steven said. "Sorry." He couldn't count the number of times he'd had to apologize to Jill since he met her.

"Well, thanks for coming by," she said, walking over toward the front door.

"No problem," Steven said. He watched Jill's face carefully to see if she really hated him, or if she was just still mad about their date. "Well, I guess I'll see you at school," he said, walking out onto the front steps.

"I guess," Jill said.

"Maybe we could go to the Dairi Burger Monday afternoon," Steven suggested. "My treat, I promise."

"I can't," Jill said. "I have other plans."

"Oh," Steven nodded. "OK, well, see you."

"Bye," Jill said. Then she shut the door, practically in Steven's face.

Steven walked down to the street to get his bicycle. It was raining even harder than before, and streams of water trickled down his neck and into his shirt. He didn't think things could get much worse. The only girl he had ever really liked didn't want to have anything to do with him.

He had to convince Jill that he wasn't a total creep, and that they belonged together. But now that he had blown it once, would she ever go out with him again?

Will Steven and Jill ever become a couple? Find out in Sweet Valley Twins and Friends #57, **BIG BROTHER'S IN LOVE!**

SWEET VALLEY TWINS™

Join Jessica and Elizabeth for
big adventure in exciting
SWEET VALLEY TWINS SUPER EDITIONS
and SWEET VALLEY TWINS CHILLERS.

☐ #1: CLASS TRIP   15588-1/$3.50
☐ #2: HOLIDAY MISCHIEF   15641-1/$3.50
☐ #3: THE BIG CAMP SECRET   15707-8/$3.50
☐ #4: THE UNICORNS GO HAWAIIAN   15948-8/$3.50
☐ SWEET VALLEY TWINS SUPER SUMMER
   FUN BOOK by Laurie Pascal Wenk   15816-3/$3.50

Elizabeth shares her favorite summer projects &
Jessica gives you pointers on parties. Plus:
fashion tips, space to record your favorite
summer activities, quizzes, puzzles, a summer
calendar, photo album, scrapbook, address book
& more!

CHILLERS

☐ #1: THE CHRISTMAS GHOST   15767-1/$3.50
☐ #2: THE GHOST IN THE GRAVEYARD
                                          15801-5/$3.50
☐ #3: THE CARNIVAL GHOST   15859-7/$2.95

The most exciting story ever
in Sweet Valley history

FRANCINE
PASCAL'S

SWEET
VALLEY
Saga

THE SWEET VALLEY SAGA tells the incredible story of the lives and
times of five generations of brave and beautiful young women who
were Jessica and Elizabeth's ancestors. Their story is the story of
America: from the danger of the pioneering days to the glamour of the
roaring nineties, the sacrifice and romance of World War II to the
rebelliousness of the Sixties, right up to the present-day Sweet Valley.
A dazzling novel of unforgettable lives and love both lost and won, THE
SWEET VALLEY SAGA is Francine Pascal's most memorable,
exciting, and wonderful Sweet Valley book ever.

BANTAM
NEW YORK • TORONTO • LONDON • SYDNEY • AUCKLAND

☐ 15927-5 **ELIZABETH THE**
            IMPOSSIBLE #51 $2.99

☐ 15933-X **BOOSTER**
            BOYCOTT #52 $2.99

☐ 15935-6 **THE SLIME THAT ATE**
            SWEET VALLEY #53 $2.99

☐ 15952-6 **THE BIG PARTY**
            WEEKEND #54 $2.99

☐ 15965-8 **BROOKE AND HER**
            ROCK-STAR MOM #55 $2.99

Bantam Books, Dept. SVT8, 2451 S. Wolf Road, Des Plaines, IL 60018

Please send me the items I have checked above. I am enclosing $_____
(please add $2.50 to cover postage and handling). Send check or money
order, no cash or C.O.D.s please.

Mr/Ms _____

Address _____

City/State _____ Zip _____

Please allow four to six weeks for delivery.   SVT8-1/92
Prices and availability subject to change without notice.